T5-DHD-936

BIGFOOT SABOTAGE

Deirdre Kessler

RAGWEED
THE ISLAND PUBLISHER

Cover & Book Art: JoDee Samuelson
Comic Strip: Hannah Felix
Printed & Bound in Canada by: Hignell Printing Ltd.
Second Printing 1993

Ragweed Press acknowledges the generous support of The Canada Council. The author also wishes to thank the P.E.I. Council of the Arts for its kind support.

Acknowledgements: "Teddy Bears' Picnic," lyrics by Jimmy Kennedy, music by John W. Bratton, © 1907, 1947, Warner Bros.; "Dig a Hole in the Meadow," from *The Folk Songs of North America*, arranged by Alan Lomax.

Published by:
Ragweed Press
P.O. Box 2023
Charlottetown, P.E.I.
Canada C1A 7N7

Canadian Cataloguing in Publication Data
Kessler, Deirdre
    Bigfoot Sabotage
    ISBN 0-921556-19-5
1. Sasquatch — Juvenile Fiction. I. Title.
PS8571.E77B54 1991 jC813'.54 C91-097654-6
PZ7.K57Bi 1991

To

Taya & Eric & Jubal

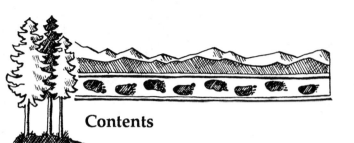

Contents

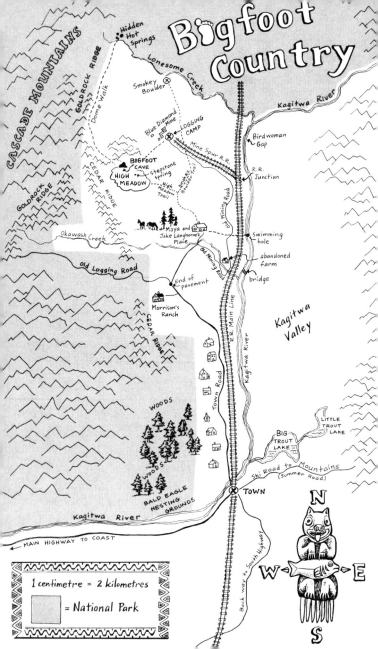

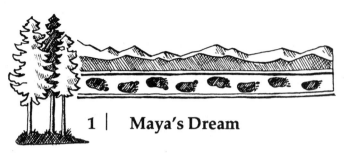

1 | Maya's Dream

"Tonight I fly."

Maya lay on her back, legs stretched out straight, arms at her side. She stared at the shadow on the wall opposite her bed. The moon was high enough to cast its light against the Douglas fir by the barn. The shadow of that tree on her wall was as familiar to Maya as anything else in her life—her mother and father, Jake, the farm, the forest. The shadow of that fir was the centre of many thoughts and dreams.

"Tonight I fly," Maya murmured. Her eyes lingered in the shadow branches of the big old tree. There was a branch high up where she often rested her eyes, imagining herself sitting there. In daylight, as many times as Maya passed that same tree, she never thought of it in the way as she did at night.

"Tonight I ... " Maya felt herself slide from the bed and glide towards the shadow tree. As she approached it her mind was thinking, "It's not the right direction—this is only a shadow on a wall .... " But then her mind quieted and she glided into the tree and sat on the branch high above the ground. She gazed around the farmyard, at the house with its solitary light coming from the living room window, where her parents sat reading in easy chairs.

"I can fly!"

Maya looked towards the back pasture and up the mountain trail where she and Jake planned to hike the next day. Effortlessly she left the Douglas fir and flew over the pasture. She looked back, and from this height the house and outbuildings seemed toylike.

Stay close to the ground and don't go too fast at first. Those were the guidelines for dream-flying she and Jake had read about in a book on lucid dreaming. Maya tingled with excitement. She willed herself up the mountain trail.

"I'll go a little higher. A little bit higher and a little bit faster!"

Maya's excitement grew. In the moonlight, the trail below was visible much as a stream is visible from a low-flying airplane.

"I wish Jake were here! This is .... " Maya found it difficult to concentrate on word-thoughts and manoeuver at the same time. She realized she was flying barely over the tops of the trees, and worried that her nightshirt would snag on a branch.

"Okay. Higher. I'm dreaming. I can go higher. I can fly."

Slowly she increased her altitude.

In no time, Maya was at the top of the trail, hovering over a high meadow. Here, moonlight shone on the flat surface, creating a pool of light in the dark forest. The still water of a little spring on the far side of the meadow brightly reflected the moon. Maya flew over the spring. A swath of moonlight invited her into the forest. She flew easily, turning, veering, soaring around tall trees until she came to a clearing. There, at the edge of the moonlit clearing, was a cave.

Maya glided to an uprooted tree. She landed silently, and just as silently walked towards the cave. Only it seemed as though her feet really did not touch the ground. It was a springy kind of walk, the way people walked on the moon—bounding, bouncing from one foot to another.

Moving her head close to the cave's mouth, Maya listened. A wave of warmth came from the dark interior. She leaned closer, and found herself gliding in, sliding into the cave, and floating towards the back wall where there seemed to be a nest of sticks and grasses.

There, curled together in a warm heap, were the creatures.

"They're bears," Maya whispered, recoiling. "They're big black bears."

Then she saw a little one lying comfortably on top of its parents, its legs and feet sprawled, its face pointed towards her.

"It's ... it's a sasquatch! A bigfoot—it's a baby bigfoot!"

Her desire was to pick it up, to hold it, to cuddle it. Unconsciously, Maya reached out to touch the soft furry baby. Its eyes opened and focused on her as she approached. It gurgled and held out its hands.

At the moment of contact she awoke.

2 | The High Meadow

"How about here?"

"Yeah, this is perfect. We'll be able to see down the gorge."

Maya and Jake swung off their backpacks and dug out their lunch. They were hungry after the long, uphill hike. They'd left home right after their chores and breakfast, when the sun had not yet risen above the tall fir trees behind their farm.

Strangers often remarked how unusual it was for a sister and brother to be best friends, but to Maya and Jake it was not remarkable at all. Not when you lived in the wilderness, five kilometres from the nearest neighbours and fourteen kilometres to school on a bus that often could not make it down your unpaved road. With less than a year separating them in age, Jake and Maya Langhorne had many interests in common. They both loved horses and they both loved hiking.

There had been summers when they had not been such good friends as they were now. Maya called it "the brat factor" and Jake called it "the boss factor." They had bickered and fought nearly their entire sixth summer, the one after Maya's first year in school when Jake had been left at home, miserable and alone, while Maya entered a whole new world from which he had been excluded. And they could barely stand one another's company during their tenth summer, after Jake's two weeks alone in the city with their aunt.

"You know, this would be a good place for our overnighter, Maya. We could pitch the tents by that little bush and build our fire on these rocks."

"And we could tether the horses there." Maya pointed into the grassy meadow which spread away from the granite cliff at their feet.

Sister and brother sat on the sunny terrace of rock and ate their sandwiches, passing a canteen of water between them. The day was growing hot. A cicada filled the air with its shrill buzzing. Jake stretched out on the rock with his hands behind his head, and closed his eyes. Maya picked up the canteen and walked into the meadow.

"I'll see if there's a spring. Wouldn't that be perfect for the horses?"

"Unh-huh," mumbled Jake.

A lavender-blue butterfly flitted among the grasses. Maya trailed it, bending low whenever it alighted to get a closer look at its markings. Only the occasional songs of white-throats and meadowlarks broke the midsummer silence. There wasn't a breeze. The stillness made Maya aware of herself and aware of everything around her as though it were super-real.

Slowly she scanned the perimeter of the meadow. The bordering trees were enormous, centuries old. Spotting a cluster of rocks near the meadow's edge, Maya picked her way through wild grasses until she came to a patch of spongy earth. And there was a spring! It was a clear pool no more than a metre wide, with an arrangement of rocks along one side of it, flat rocks which almost seemed placed there by a human hand.

Maya knelt and drank the cool water. She splashed some on her face. Sitting on her heels, she observed how the water trickled away from the spring on the side where there were no rocks, seeped into the clumps of grass, and disappeared. She filled the canteen and stood.

There was something uncanny about this high meadow, something Maya couldn't quite pinpoint. She wasn't fearful. After all, it was broad daylight. But she had the sense of being watched or of being in a place where perhaps she needed an invitation to be. And she had the oddest sense of having been in this exact spot before.

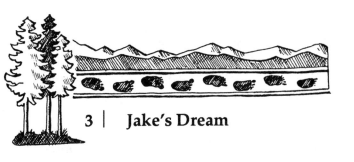

3 | Jake's Dream

Jake lay comfortably on the warm terrace of rock with his Stetson over his face—his gen-u-ine Stetson, as he always called it. No matter how rushed he was, Jake always said, "Where's my gen-u-ine Stetson," not, "Where's my hat?"

The mountain slanted away below him to a stretch of forest—thousands of hectares of forest which never had been logged. Jake's muscles ached. The sun-warmed rocks felt good against his back. He had been earning extra money by splitting wood, and had outdone himself this past week. Three neat rows of fragrant red cedar were his reward. Maya, too, had been working hard, tending two new horses they were boarding for the summer. With each load of manure she wheeled to the garden from the compost heap by the barn she would say, "That little effort will buy another bale of hay for the winter." The money she and Jake earned from their extra jobs paid for their own horses' upkeep. Both of them were saving to buy new saddles.

Jake felt himself drifting into a delicious sleep. Just before he dropped off he muttered, "Today I fly. Today I fly."

In the book on dream-flying he and Maya had found, the directions were to practise flying during sleep first by flying slowly and low to the ground. The way to set up the experience was to say, "tonight I fly," just before falling asleep. There was a warning about the dangers of flying too fast or too high before a person got the hang of it.

"Today I fly."

Jake was aware of himself lying on the rocks overlooking the mountainside and he also was aware of sliding sideways and slowly turning over so that he was on his belly. Then, in slow motion, he eased off the rock and cruised down the cliff, hovering just a metre above the ground. He observed plants which grew from crevices in the rocks. He saw a colony of ants busy at work excavating a new addition to their home. He drifted past a Steller's jay preening in a low bush.

When the jay didn't scare up as he passed, Jake was aware that he was flying. He was tickled.

"Look at me, Maya! I'm flying!" As soon as the words were out of his mouth he realized that Maya would not be able to see or hear him because he was down over the cliff. He willed himself to change directions. Slowly, slowly he turned and began to fly up over the ledge, where he could see himself still lying asleep on the rocks.

"What a blast!" he laughed. "I'm sleeping and I'm also flying."

Giving himself a boost, he soared up and flew across the meadow towards Maya. He felt the warmth of earth air against his cheek and breathed in the sunny fragrance of the wildflowers and grasses.

Maya stood mesmerized by the spring. A shiver ran down her spine. Shaking herself, again she scanned the perimeter of the field. Her eyes rested for a moment on Jake, asleep on the flat rocks, and then followed the curve of the meadow around to the dense forest.

"I'm up here, Maya. Look at me!"

Jake flitted back and forth over Maya's head, gaining in his ability to veer and turn, and increasing speed at each pass over her head.

Maya slung the canteen over her shoulder and started back across the meadow. Jake knew she would wake him when she returned, so he decided to have a quick look around. He flew to the edge of the field and flitted in and among the giant firs and hemlocks.

Not more than several hundred metres into the woods was a rocky outcrop. A gigantic uprooted tree provided a break in the density of the growth. Jake flew close to the blowdown and to his delight saw the dark opening of a large cave. Just as he lowered his altitude to approach the mouth of the cave, a form appeared. First its shoulders and head, then, with a grunt, the figure stood.

"It's a bear!" Jake whispered. Unconsciously he turned and flew upward, to put a safe distance between himself and the monster.

"It's a huge black bear and it's carrying a little baby. This is too much."

Another form appeared from the cave and went close to the first one. It took the baby bear and set it in a patch of sunlight near the cave mouth.

Remembering his dream state, Jake dropped lower to get a better look.

"It's not a bear. They're not bears," he said aloud. "They're ... they're sasquatch!"

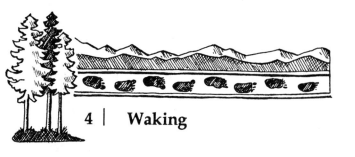

4 | Waking

"There's something strange about this place, Jake. Jake?"

Jake was soundly asleep underneath his gen-u-ine Stetson. It was unusual for either of them to sleep during the day, though Maya also felt weary from the double load of barn work she had been doing. She sat near Jake and leaned against an upright rock.

"Uh, uh," grunted Jake, waking. "Maya, uh, I gotta .... Uh, this is .... there's a .... Wait a minute."

With some difficulty Jake pulled himself to a sitting position and rubbed his eyes and his face.

"You're stunned."

"You won't believe it, Maya ... "

"I believe it. You're as stunned as a bag of hammers." Maya always thought it was funny to watch people when they first awoke, when language and movement made them act like aliens.

"No, really. Listen. There are creatures .... Uh ... uh, this is too much."

Jake stood, his body still half-asleep, but his mind racing. He looked across the meadow and into the woods where he had just been in his dream.

A fleeting image niggled at the edge of Maya's awareness—an odd familiarity with the high field, a sense that something had happened here that she should know about. And it was all strangely tied to Jake's mumbling, his weird state of half-sleep. If only she could remember. There was something ....

"In the woods, Maya. Oh, this is too much .... A mother and a father and a baby. Right over there."

Maya was floating now, remembering her dream, almost remembering what it was she had seen.

"I saw them." Jake's voice had lost any edge of sleep now. "I was dream flying and I saw them."

Maya scrutinized Jake's face. She knew him well. Sometimes he played elaborate jokes on her, but right now he was serious. His eyes had a certain look, holding in focus something he had just seen, something incredible, something he had never before seen.

Maya stared into Jake's eyes and suddenly she, too, saw.

"I remember!" she exhaled. "I saw them, too. Bigfeet!"

A chill spread over them both. Fear and excitement, rolled up together.

"Tell me."

Jake explained how he had set up his nap for flying and had seen the sasquatch family outside their cave. He described the creatures in detail, but it was his description of the spring that caught Maya's attention. She knew he had been lying on the rocks the whole time she was exploring the meadow so it would have been impossible for him to have seen the little spring with its flatrock border.

Then Maya described her dream.

Jake took a swig of water from the canteen and put on his backpack. Maya did likewise. Without speaking, the two set off across the meadow towards the spring.

5 | Home Sweet Home

"Why aren't there tracks all around, Maya?"

They were crossing the drainage field of the spring. "Look at the imprints we've made. And there are tracks of elk. And raccoon. And .... "

"I bet they walk on the rocks." Maya hurried ahead. "They probably use the spring from the other side."

Brother and sister edged around the spring, walking on the flatrock border and then going from stone to stone into the shady growth of the ancient forest which had grown up around this trail of giant stepping stones left behind by a glacier. It was possible to keep walking on rocks until they were well under the canopy of tall trees.

"I came in through the break in the trees, and flew this way," Jake whispered.

"That's how I came in, too. The cave's just over there. Just .... "

And there it was. Maya and Jake crouched and stared wide-eyed at the dark cave at the far side of a clearing created by an upturned tree, a blowdown from a past storm. The forest was strangely still. In the gloom of the conifers no insects whirred. Birds were silent.

"Let's get behind that root," Jake breathed more than whispered. "We'll be able to see into the cave."

Stealthily they moved to the massive blowdown. Humus and clay still clung to most of the exposed root system. One large root, waist height from the ground, had a smooth, curved section. Maya and Jake inched forward, scarcely breathing.

A frantic chattering broke the silence. A red squirrel had spotted them and was announcing their presence to the woodland world. It ran crazily up a nearby tree, crossed over to another by a maze of dead branches, and fixed them with its shiny eyes.

"Dang," whispered Jake.

Circling in the trees surrounding their hiding place, the squirrel kept up its alarm.

"If we act as though we belong here," Maya said, "it'll settle when it sees we're not going to harm it. Let's play rock and scissors. That always works."

Silently Maya and Jake shook their fists in the hand game they had learned to help pass the time on long journeys in the backseat of the family's car.

"Paper covers rock," Maya whispered. "That's one to nothing. Rock smashes scissors. That's two to nothing."

"Hah! Scissors cut paper! Two to one."

After a few minutes the squirrel moved on.

Maya picked up a stone and aimed carefully. The stone landed inside the cave.

"Good shot."

Jake found a stone and threw it. His landed with a crack against the cave entrance and ricocheted into the cave.

"I don't think they've come back yet," Jake whispered.

Sister and brother crept across the clearing.

"Hello ... is anybody home?" Maya stuck her head into the cave mouth.

Jake glanced behind them and did the same. "Hello?"

They took a few steps into the cave.

"I smell something," said Maya. "Look— there's the edge of something. It's ... a nest."

"Look here." Jake had found a corner filled with pine cones and small brown nuts.

"It goes further back—look, Jake. Look how far back it goes. We need a flashlight."

"I think we'd better leave." Jake stepped back to the cave entrance and nervously looked into the forest. "Maya, let's go."

Blinking when the sunlight hit her eyes, Maya emerged from the cave.

"When I saw them come out, they had to duck down." Jake stretched his hand over the cave entrance, estimating the height of the bigfeet when they stood. "They've got to be at least this big."

Maya took off her backpack, pulled out a sack, and quickly dumped its contents of un-shelled peanuts near the mouth of the cave.

"It's not really nice of us to invade their home," she said. "We'll leave them something so they'll know we're friendly."

All the way back down the trail to their farm, Maya and Jake were silent. After supper they retreated to their rooms and went to bed early.

6 | Fire!

"Maya! Jake! Wake up! Get up! There's a fire at the Morrison Ranch. Get your gear. We'll load the truck."

Stan and Lydia Langhorne were tossing burlap bags into the back of the pickup when Maya and Jake stumbled outside, carrying their work boots and heavy socks.

"I'll ride in back," said Jake. He had his eye on the pile of burlap bags. In a moment he had rearranged the chainsaw, shovels and axes, and had spread out the extra pairs of overalls on top of a heap of burlap bags to make himself a bed.

Maya climbed into the cab. "What happened?"

"Must have started in their east field by the road," Lydia said. "Everything's so dry. Maybe someone tossed a cigarette. Wind took it into the woods and now there's a shift and the barn's in danger."

Maya woke completely on the word *barn*. She scrambled back out of the pickup and ran into their own barn.

"Maya! We're ready! Come on!" Stan was behind the wheel. Lydia had made a final dash to the house for a jug of water and a bunch of bananas and was sliding across the seat next to Stan when Maya reappeared with a handful of leather straps and a bucket. She tossed them into the back and climbed next to Lydia.

The Morrison ranch lay at the foot of Cedar Ridge. Behind it was the forest and the mountains. The house and outbuildings were nestled against the ridge, facing south. To the east, south, and west lay some of the nicest pastureland in the county. The Morrisons' farm was the only piece of land south of Okawash Creek which did not belong to the National Park.

It took Stan far less time than it did the school bus to travel the five kilometres from the Langhornes' place to the Morrisons'. The Langhorne house lay on the north side of Okawash Creek, just past the bend in Blue Diamond Road. It was a convenient layout. From the house they could see any cars which passed the end of the lane—not that there generally was much traffic along the old mine road. Because the Langhornes were the last residents on the road, the school bus turned around using their lane. Sometimes Maya and Jake would see the bus turn in and they would make a mad dash down the lane to catch it. They would not have minded missing school, but the Langhorne house rule on the subject was strict: it was their own responsibility to get to school on time or pay the consequences, which outweighed the pleasure of a day off.

Stan had both hands on the wheel and sat intently upright. The first three kilometres were unpaved and pocked with potholes from spring run-off. Jake gave up trying to prolong his night's sleep and held on to the truck sides to keep himself from pitching out and onto the road. When they reached the pavement and Stan accelerated even faster, Jake let out a whoop.

"Ride 'em cowboy!" he shouted. He loved it when Stan and Lydia broke the speed limit. Unfortunately this happened only when there were emergencies, which detracted somewhat from the thrill.

The Morrisons' main barn stood by itself in the pasture a distance from the house and fairly close to the town road. Smoke curved in a swath across their east field and into the forest. The siren from the town's firetruck could be heard in the distance, and one of the county's yellow earthmovers was just pulling up to the gathering crowd. Already there were a number of cars and trucks parked along the road.

Maya and Jake spent the last few moments of the approach tucking their pantlegs into their socks and lacing up their boots.

"Johnnie—can you doze a line from the old logging road in towards the house and then angle east into the field? Fire's gone into the woods."

Alec Morrison had a wild look about him, but his voice was calm.

"Stan, if you and Bud take your chainsaws and follow Johnnie, you could clear any trees the Cat might have trouble with."

"Fire department'll wet the field by the house. But we'd better get to shovelling and beating around the barn. Horses are in the paddock. Kids may be having trouble getting close enough to put halters on them."

Alec's eye caught and acknowledged Maya, who had two halters over her shoulder and was shaking loose the lead ropes.

"Thanks, Maya. Go around the north side of the barn. Smoke's not too bad yet."

Jake grabbed his shovel and the bucket of oats and trotted by Maya's side to join Karen and Sam in the paddock. They could see Nina Morrison and several neighbours beating at a line of flames not far from the barn.

Within minutes everyone knew where best to help. Fire was a serious business. It had been an unusually dry spring, and summer had brought fears of drought. A copy of the telephone tree for emergencies was posted and kept up-to-date in every single farmhouse and cabin in the valley.

Lotta, the faithful donkey, stood inside the paddock gate, halter on, waiting patiently to be led out and away from the smoke. But the two horses careened frantically in the small enclosure with Karen and Sam trailing them, trying unsuccessfully to get ropes around them. Maya and Jake let themselves into the paddock.

"Good girl, Lotta. Want some grain?" Maya took a handful of grain from the bucket held by Jake. Lotta ate it and hunted for more. "Let's move her to the centre," Maya murmured.

Karen and Sam stopped their desperate chase and came to Maya and Jake.

"Just stand here and talk to Lotta," Maya said calmly. She took the bucket and began to shake it. "Come on, Sienna. Here Bess. Come on." Halter over her shoulder, the rope in one hand and the bucket in the other, Maya slowly moved away from the little gathering around the donkey. She rattled the grain in the pail and continued talking in low tones. The mare and gelding slackened their frenzied pace somewhat and kept their eyes on Maya as they charged back and forth in the paddock.

Jake admired Maya's way with horses, though at first he had been jealous of her skill.

"What's the deal with horses and girls?" he had asked her, miffed that she could always approach, catch, and saddle both of their horses with ease. "How come horses put their ears back around me? I don't beat them or mistreat them. I mean, what is it? It's almost as though they think you're a horse, too."

"I don't know," Maya had answered. "Boys walk differently than girls. And sometimes boys use their elbows in a way that makes horses nervous. I don't know, Jake. Maybe boys smell different. Or maybe girls need animal friends more than boys do."

Jake had begun to experiment, to imitate the way Maya talked and moved around the horses, and he had noticed changes, noticed the horses were growing more trusting with him.

"Here, Bess. That's it. Here's some nice grain. Bet you haven't had oats since winter. Here, girl."

Bess halted and stood wide-legged, nostrils flared, eyes nervously flicking between Maya and the fingers of flame which had found patches of long grass around the paddock fence posts. She hesitated, but was drawn to the circle of calm. Tentatively, Bess stretched her head towards the pail of grain. Maya set the pail on the ground and lifted a heaping handful. As soon as Bess shoved her nose close to the pail, Maya had the rope around her neck. It was easy to put the halter on and click the lead shank into place. Karen handed Maya the second halter and took Bess. Seeing his mate standing calmly, Sienna ventured towards Maya, who caught him in a similar fashion.

Jake grabbed a shovel and began to beat out the paddock fire. Maya, Karen and Sam led Lotta and the horses out of the paddock and down the road. They tied them inside an abandoned machine shed, and ran back to help the brigade which was working to keep the barn from catching fire.

The fire truck rolled into the pasture and its crew hosed down the windward side of the barn. Everyone worked, digging, throwing dirt on the flames, chasing the fire as it leapt from patch to patch of long grass. With burlap sacks they beat out small blazes and kept the main line of fire away from the barn. The wind helped them this time, and quieted, so that before long the fire had nowhere new to burn along the front line and so it burned backwards and burned itself out.

"We did it!"

Nina Morrison stood, sooty and sweaty, surveying the field. Shovels in hand, the firefighters gathered around her by the barn. "A couple of us can stay here to make sure the field doesn't flare up again. The rest can go help in the forest."

Jake and Maya piled into a pick-up with half a dozen others and drove up the old logging road where the second crew had gone. By now the park service would have heard about the fire and more help would be en route. There was no other access to this part of the forest. It would be serious if the fire got out of hand and burned over the mountain.

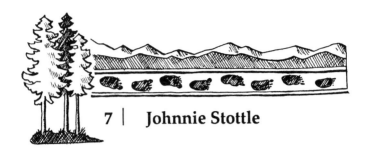

7 | Johnnie Stottle

"Hey, Stottle, you still got your tee-shirt on even when it's off!"

Johnnie laughed. He didn't take off his shirt very often. It was cooler keeping it on. His neck and arms where the shirt stopped were permanently tanned. Underneath he was white. The same thing with his head. He always wore his cap pulled down over his forehead so he got a good slant on the earth he was moving. The line where white skin met tan ran across his forehead at a slight angle. It was not noticeable when his face was dusty and sweaty from the day's work, but after his evening shower and on weekends in the bar he took a lot of ribbing from the rest of the gang.

When Johnnie Stottle had been a kid in elementary school, he had stuttered and the other children had made fun of him.

Hey, hey, hey, J-johnnie St-stottle
Drinks sour milk from a b-baby b-bottle.

Maybe that was why he never had much use for talking, even when the stutter disappeared.

Johnnie Stottle quit school in grade nine and got working papers. He lied, said he was sixteen, claimed he had a driver's licence, said his daddy owned a Cat. And when he climbed onto his first 926E and sat in the high padded seat that first morning of his first real job, Johnnie Stottle came home. He started the engine of the big diesel earthmover, put it in gear, and drove off, smooth as marbles. He never stuttered again.

Johnnie had driven up the logging road by Okawash Creek and turned into the forest behind the Morrisons' ranch. Neat as could be he manoeuvered the Caterpillar through the trees, clipping the odd branch or small tree with a calculated swerve so the bucket took out the obstruction. Occasionally he would stop, back up, and make a second run. He sussed out the lay of the land, the wind shift, the path of flames and, with the help of Stan and the others, cut off the fire. A little backtracking and earthmoving to smother flare-ups, and the job was done.

Maya and Jake and the barn brigade arrived to see a group standing around Johnnie's yellow machine. After the emergency, there was a sense of comraderie and mutual accomplishment that everyone wanted to prolong. There was speculation about what the fire could have done and stories of past fires. Talk eventually turned to local news.

"Yep," said Johnnie, "I'm quittin' the county Monday. I'll be drivin' a 657E push-pull scraper for old man Sidder. Brand new. We're clearin' the other side of Okawash Creek."

Johnnie looked north towards the creek that ran by the Langhornes' place, a creek whose fresh waters tumbled from the mountains which lay to the west, protecting the valley. "Right through there as the crow flies, I reckon."

Stan's body stiffened and his voice lost the glow of satisfaction they all felt from keeping the fire from damaging their beloved forest.

"But that's watershed land, Johnnie. You're not serious. Sidder can't clearcut that forest. National Park's going to buy that land. It's protected. Or will be. He's got no right to clearcut."

"That's all I know," Johnnie said, setting his cap down on the dozer. He pulled a wadded tee-shirt from his back pocket, put it on, and replaced his cap. "All I know is I got a job startin' a week Monday. Pays twice what the county gives me. Takin' a week's holidays so Mama can visit her sister in Calgary. Sidder owns that land and I guess he figures he can do what he wants with it. Ain't my business to discuss his rights."

Johnnie swung up into the cab. "Well, guess I'll be gettin' back to the county yard so I can stand around and do nothin'."

Alec Morrison reached up to shake hands with Johnnie. "Really appreciate your help, son. We couldn't have done it without you. Thanks."

Johnnie Stottle hated any kind of formality. He blushed, though his face was so sun-reddened no one noticed, nodded his head, and put the machine in gear. Everyone watched as Johnnie neatly turned the earthmover around and jounced onto the logging road and headed back to town.

"Well, everything's out down below," Nina Morrison said. "Thank you, one and all. How about coming back to the house for coffee and some breakfast—I've got a whole flat of huckleberries waiting to jump into pancake batter."

The good mood was restored. Sidder & Company's plans to clearcut slid into the background as friends and neighbours loaded into various vehicles and returned to the Morrison ranch.

Later, when they were back home, Lydia made several telephone calls. Her part-time job with *The Kagitwa Valley Times* gave her access to many sources of information.

"You were right, Stan. Sidder can't clearcut up there. When he bought that tract of land from Blue Diamond Mine, the National Park had already negotiated a covenant because that's all watershed for the Valley. The covenant says no one can clear the forest south of Narnauk Peak to the bend in the Kagitwa River and east of the Cascades to Goldrock Ridge. The river drains that whole area and all our ground water is affected by those slopes.

"Evidently, the National Park wanted the land, too, but Sidder got it first. So Sidder can strip cut or selection cut only. He's planning to get the old mine road in shape and start logging. That's Johnnie's new job, to widen Blue Diamond Mine Road and clear a logging camp area."

Maya and Jake looked at each other. They were thinking the same thought.

"What exactly does Sidder own?" Maya asked. "You know the high meadow at the top of our back trail? Does Sidder own that?"

Stan got a map from the living room and spread it out on the table. "See this square of land? Sidder owns it all except our place and the abandoned farm at the end of our road. His land is bordered on the north by Lonesome Creek, right here. And on the south by

Okawash Creek that runs by our place. The west side of his land stops at Goldrock Ridge. And the Kagitwa River runs down the east side. Pretty much of a square patch of forest. The National Park surrounds him on three sides. Wonder if Sidder owns the forest on the east side of the Kagitwa, too. Why else would he go to the expense of building a road just to log a couple of hundred hectares?"

"Eliot heard Sidder's lawyers may have found a loophole in the covenant and are going to court." Lydia slid her arm around Maya's shoulders and with her other hand pushed Jake's hair off his brow. Sometimes Lydia had a snapshot view of her little family, and it squeezed her heart. She felt as though she were reading about her life, or making it up—how different all this was from her own experience of growing up.

"Well, I'm relieved, anyway," Stan sighed. "At least he can't clearcut the slopes. That would be something. Move all the way up here to get away from the city, fix up a peaceful place, and just when we've got everything the way we like it, down comes a mud slide to cover us. Just like what happened after the east side of Rainbow Mountain was clearcut."

Jake was studying the map carefully. His fingers traced the area around the high meadow where he and Maya had found the bigfoot cave.

"Pop, what's the difference between strip and selection cutting?" he asked.

"Well, selection cutting means they take only the mature, dead or overmature trees and leave the rest. That way younger trees have more light and room to grow. Strip cutting, well, they clear a whole patch of timber. Log all the worthwhile stuff, leave big piles of slash and rubble. Then skip a patch—leave it alone—and log the next patch. Like a checkerboard. Though, if they see good timber up there, they take it. No one really patrols when the companies are so far back in the wilderness. National Park might be nosy, though."

Jake and Maya exchanged glances. Little strands of anxiety twisted and knotted inside them. Both had a vague, heavy feeling that something was wrong, that something awful was going to happen, though they had no clear idea what it might be.

8 | Tonight We Fly

"Maya, are you asleep?"

"No, come on in."

Jake tiptoed into Maya's room and sat on the end of her bed. "I can't sleep. I keep thinking about the bigfoot family. Do you think they're real?"

"I don't know. They sure seemed real. And we did find the nest. Cripes, I hate the thought of Sidder doing any logging in there. He'll mess up Lonesome Creek and Smokey Boulder. And the Dome Walk. And there's plenty of good timber right around the bigfoot cave. It makes me sick."

"Yeah, me too." Jake slid his feet under Maya's comforter and leaned against the wall. "We should scout the old mine road and see where Johnnie's going to put the logging camp. Surveyors'll be in there first."

Maya sat up. "And then we could ride from the camp back towards the bigfoot cave, to see if it's likely they'd get to it."

"Yeah. Maybe there're canyons or ridges they couldn't build roads through. Maybe they can't even get to the cave area to log it!"

Maya and Jake were pleased with themselves. Now that they had a plan of action they no longer felt helpless. They'd get their chores done early the next day and then exercise the horses on Blue Diamond road. If they pushed it, they could reach the mine and then find a path to the bigfoot cave. If the terrain was inaccessible, they'd return home on the old mine road. If they made it to the bigfoot cave, they could come home down the high field trail.

"Jake—we should dream fly tonight. Go see if there really are bigfeet. Maybe it was flukey that we both dreamed we saw them."

"Yeah. And you know what?" Jake was thinking aloud. His voice took on a dreamy quality and even in the darkness Maya could see by his posture that he was hatching a plan.

"What? Jake—what it is?"

"Well, we could dream fly together! We could both be there! All we need to do is agree to meet someplace inside the dream. Remember what the book said? If we find a common point in our dreams and concentrate on it .... "

Maya picked up where Jake left off. " ... and say aloud where we're going and who we're going to meet. Okay! Let's meet at that uprooted tree, the one closest to the cave.

Remember how one of the big roots had a dip in it?"

"Yeah—like a sitting place! Good idea. We'll meet there. We'll go right to the sitting root and look for each other."

Jake scrambled off Maya's bed and headed for his own room. "Good-night, Maya. Tonight we fly!"

"Night, Jake. See you later."

"Tonight I fly. Tonight I fly. This is Maya. I am going to the bigfoot cave and I am meeting Jake at the sitting root. Tonight I fly."

Maya's heart raced with excitement. Sleep seemed the last thing she wanted to or could do. The moments dragged on. Finally she decided to calm herself by counting branches on the shadow tree. It was an old habit. She had never been able to count to the top of the tree before sleep had overtaken her.

" ... eleven, twelve, thir-teen, four-teen, fif-teen, six- ...."

The magic of counting worked. Maya felt herself drifting into the halfway land between waking and sleep. Just as she went over the edge, she murmured, "Tonight I fly." She thought she started to say aloud where and with whom she was going, when an awareness of herself separating from her body took over. She oozed out of the screened window and floated up over the farm. Moving much faster than she had during the previous flight, she whizzed up the trail to the high meadow. Over the spring she dropped altitude and darted in and among the trees towards the cave. At the uprooted tree she bounced to a landing and placed her hands on the curve of the sitting root. Jake was nowhere to be seen.

Maya's attention was drawn to activity at the cave mouth where the mother bigfoot was wiping the baby bigfoot's face. The baby squirmed and kicked with its enormous feet. Little tufts of hair stood straight up on the baby's head. It looked like a furry punker. Maya laughed. The baby turned towards her and looked straight into her eyes. Maya held out her arms—oh, how she wanted to hold this little creature. In a moment, the baby bigfoot had pulled away from its mother and run to Maya. With a gurgle and a squeal it jumped into her arms and clung to her. How soft it was, and how strong! It wrapped its legs around her waist and its arms around her neck. Maya felt its feet with her hands. The baby gurgled again and kicked, as though its feet were ticklish.

"You little punk," Maya cooed. "You're just a furry little punkster!"

A series of low grunts and whistles made the baby stop its playful squirming and look towards the cave. In a flash it unwrapped itself from Maya, jumped to the ground, and ran back to the mother. Its pigeon-toed, tumbling gait made Maya laugh. The father bigfoot came out of the cave, swung the baby up onto his shoulder, and the three of them set off in a northerly direction, away from the meadow. Neither of the grown bigfeet seemed to see her.

Without the slowness and hindrance of thought, Maya knew they were headed towards Blue Diamond Mine. She effortlessly floated up and flew along behind them, keeping a respectful distance. From time to time the baby would spot her and twist around on its father's shoulder to wave and gurgle at her.

From the cave the bigfoot family followed a deer path which brought them onto Goldrock Ridge. They followed the ridge to Lonesome Creek and walked in the creek for a short while before coming to a rocky ledge overhanging the creek. The bigfeet hoisted themselves onto the ledge and crossed to a series of steaming pools. The water of the hot springs flowed from one pool to another and then tumbled down a steep crevice and out of view. The family lounged in the pools, splashing happily, dipping their heads under water and shaking wildly. Maya watched them in fascination.

After a while, she began to explore the area. She cruised down the crevice, through a narrow gap, following the little stream of tumbling water which made its way around gigantic boulders and upheavals of rock eons old. A kilometre below the pools where the bigfoot family bathed, Maya came to Lonesome Creek again. The water from the hidden hot springs emptied into the creek. Most likely, no one had ever found the springs because here the creek flowed through a narrow gap surrounded by jutting, inhospitable formations of granite.

Maya willed herself to fly higher than she had gone before. Below her, she could see how the land lay, and that the Dome Walk was part of an ancient trail along Goldrock Ridge between the bigfoot cave and the hot springs. The trail went on, leading north along Goldrock Ridge towards Narnauk Peak, one of the highest points of land on the continent. To the south, the trail veered west across Okawash Creek and continued towards the coast. It occurred to Maya that she could see everything, as plain as day. How could it be day when it was night? And where was the sun?

"It's night-time. It's night-time. It's night ... " Maya heard herself talking and woke. With a great effort she rolled over in bed and opened her eyes. The room was dark. Shadow branches on the wall swayed stiffly. Maya hoisted herself upright in bed and looked out the window. The night had grown cloudy and the wind was picking up. Maya could smell rain. She looked at the clock. It was three in the morning. What had she been dreaming? What was it? She felt tired, as though she had done a hard day's work. Her thoughts would not untangle. She lay back in bed, pulled the warm comforter around her chin, and fell into a deep, dreamless sleep.

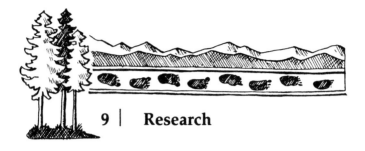

"Sleep much?"

"What?"

"Sleep is for the weak."

Maya pulled her face out of the feather pillow, reluctantly leaving the warmth and softness and scent of slumber. She sat up and scowled at Jake.

"What?"

"It's raining."

"So."

"So, no scouting expedition."

"What?" Maya rubbed her face and looked out the window. Rain pounded straight down. It was a summer downpour, soaking everything, dripping off the eaves of the house, puddling the yard.

"What expedition?"

"Now look who's stunned as hammers." Jake had been up since dawn, scheming.

"Oh, Jake—I flew! I saw them again! The baby! But ... the root, the sitting root .... Did you dream? Did you fly?"

"Yup, I did, but it wasn't at all like the last time. I mean, I don't even remember starting off. All of a sudden I was somewhere, but it wasn't the high field and it wasn't at the big-foot cave. There was an uprooted tree, but it wasn't the one we saw. And there were lots of sitting roots. No—they were trunks of weird bent trees, not fallen ones. And there was kind of a circle of big stones, like a huge campfire, but with nothing in the centre. And there were caves all along one ridge. Just as I was floating closer, to see if maybe I could find you, all these birds swarmed around me—eagles and vultures and hawks and little birds. Dang, Maya, it was more like a real dream than the other day. Anyway, all these birds flew everywhere, as though they were gathering like geese do in the autumn. Then the birds were gone and I guess I'd kinda flown real high to get out of their way, and I saw a whole bunch of sasquatch coming from both direc-tions along the ridge, all heading towards the circle. They came in twos and threes and some-times there was a group of six or seven of them. All sizes. I remember calling out to you to come look, and then I woke up."

"Wow, what a dream! How many bigfeet?"

"I don't know. Lots. Some of them were almost white, and some were reddish, some brown, and others were like ours—like black bears. They weren't as big as movie sasquatch."

"Where was it? Did you recognize anything?"

"Nothing. I've never seen the place before."

Jake's eyes took on a distant look as he replayed the scene in his head. "Wait—remember when we all hiked up Lonesome Creek and found Smokey Boulder? I passed over that early on. I flew a long way, that much I know."

Maya was no longer sleepy. She jumped up and grabbed her clothes.

"We've got to do some research. Let's hurry and do the barn work and go to town with Ma. We can go to the library. Maybe the forestry service has aerial maps we can look at. I'll tell you my dream later."

That evening Maya and Jake lay on the living room floor pouring over maps, trying to locate the stone circle and the cave ridge Jake had seen. Maya described the trail which led from the bigfoot cave to the hidden hot springs by Lonesome Creek. They decided that Sidder's machines probably could not get in to log the area around the hot springs, and that most of the upper reaches of Lonesome Creek were rocky, with the few patches of good trees accessible only through park land. But their hearts sank as they realized that the forest around the bigfoot cave and high meadow was reachable.

"Now here's an interesting assortment of books."

Stan scanned the titles of the library books they had checked out: *Flora and Fauna of the Pacific Northwest, Harvesting the Forest, Forest Management, Field Guide to Imaginary Creatures, North American Indian Legends, The Elusive Yeti of Eastern Siberia, In Search of Sasquatch, Lock Ness and Other Monsters.*

Neither Maya nor Jake felt like discussing their dreams with Stan or Lydia. When they had asked to accompany Lydia when she went to work, they simply said they had a project and needed to use the library. Lydia asked no questions. That was one thing about their family—everyone had projects. Sometimes you talked about your projects, even got help with them, other times everyone just left you alone. That was how Lydia and Stan had made birthday desks for Maya and Jake without their knowing about it. Even if they had noticed something in the workshop, they would not have snooped. All you had to say to anybody was, "If you go in my room, don't look on the desk." Or, "I've got a project in the old shed." Or, "You know the little grove behind the barn? Don't look in there for a while." That was enough to let everybody know a certain area was off limits.

"Yeah, Pop," Jake said. "We're reading about logging and stuff."

Stan sat down at the big desk he and Lydia shared and pulled out plans he was working on for an addition to their kitchen. Stan had been born on the West Coast and loved the scale of the mountains and trees, loved the damp air, the pungent scent of cedar. The five years he had spent living in the city were bearable only because it was there he had met Lydia, the first person who ever gave him the same feeling he had when he was at home in the forest. There was something still and deep and mysterious about her, something he did not care to put into words.

Lydia wandered into the living room and settled into an overstuffed chair with one of her paperback mysteries. Lydia had a habit of exclaiming aloud every once in a while as she was reading. "Of course! Searle did it!" or "Haverstock's the one to watch!" No one ever asked what she meant. Lydia was the only person they knew who could figure out whodunits by the time she had read the first fifty pages. Asked why she bothered reading mysteries when she could solve them so easily, her answer was, "To keep in shape."

Rain droned on the roof. Outside, the world was dark and green and dripping. Inside, the family read in cosy, companionable silence.

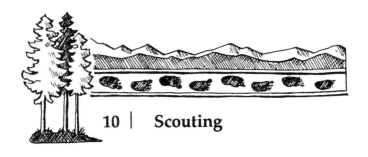

10 | Scouting

"Okay if we go up Blue Diamond Road with the horses, Ma?"

Maya had led Felix to the edge of the garden where Lydia spent most of her waking hours. Jake was saddling up Hannah in the paddock. Felix was black with a white face and four white stockings. Maya thought he looked like a big black-and-white cat, and he even had cat ways, which made him a good mountain trail horse. Hannah was a sleek dappled gray, a gentle horse who let Maya and Jake climb all over her when they played circus. Before the family had bought Felix, Maya and Jake used to ride double on barebacked Hannah.

The only rule their parents laid out for hiking and riding was that they say where they were going and when they could be expected back. Both Maya and Jake carried a survival kit in their backpacks; each knew there was no underestimating the unforeseen with horses or the wilderness.

Their usual riding trails were along the unpaved road from their house towards the Morrisons' place. Often they would meet Karen and Sam and together ride up the old logging road or along Cedar Ridge trail towards town. Sometimes they'd ride the Blue Diamond Road to the abandoned farm and up as far as the Junction, where the old Blue Diamond mine spur joined up with the railroad tracks of the main line which paralleled the Kagitwa River.

"We'll be back by lunchtime," Jake called from the lane as he swung into Hannah's saddle and headed across the little bridge in front of the Langhorne house.

After the rain, the earth smelled rich. July was an abundant month here—berries, wildflowers, little rabbits, seedlings. The danger of fire had been reduced by the good soaking, and it seemed that every creature chirped or buzzed or hopped or slithered with lifted spirits. Felix and Hannah were impatient to run. They pulled against their bits as Maya and Jake held them to a walk for the first ten minutes out.

They crossed Okawash Creek twice, in front of their ranch and back again to the north side over the bridge by the abandoned farm. At the mine spur junction they spotted the first surveyors' stakes. Here the old mine road was rutted and gullied from many years of washouts. The road angled northwest to Blue Diamond Mine, more or less paralleling the railroad spur. It was easy to see why Sidder needed to level and widen the road to move in the tree-harvesting equipment.

In a flat area below the mine camp, Maya and Jake dismounted and tied Felix and Hannah. Stakes wrapped with neon strips marked out a rectangle large enough for a number of machines to turn around in. The area had been cleared a century or so before, and the timbers were used to build the mine shaft and the camp cabins. Railroad tracks led from the mine entrance to the junction by the Kagitwa River, where the main line ran north through the Cascades and south to town and then angled west towards the coast.

Blue Diamond Mine had been defunct for years, one of many copper mines which had boomed and busted. Piles of tailings and rusted ore cars spoke of a distant era. The gray cabins were doorless and all of the glass was long gone from the windows. The cabins had been ransacked through the years. There were signs of occasional habitation by drifters—a stove still hooked up to its pipe, a few broken chairs around a weathered wooden table, an ancient mattress hauled close to a stove.

The Langhornes had explored the old mining camp nearly every summer. It held a fascination for them, as though voices of the miners and their families still rang from cabin to cabin, as though there might still be a lonesome miner stuck down in the ground, picking out ore, hauling it into the sunshine. Once they had stood in the cool gloom inside the main entrance of the mine. They had wanted to go farther, but knew it was foolish to venture any deeper into the shaft.

Felix and Hannah nickered impatiently, anxious for a gallop, but when Maya and Jake remounted, they held them in as they slowly picked their way from the mine towards Bigfoot Cave. They rode far enough to confirm what Maya had seen in her dream. The area was relatively unrocky and easily accessible. It would be a cinch for Sidder & Company to clear. This was a magnificent stand of forest. In fact, all the land to west and south as far as the Langhorne ranch was prime forest land.

The expanse of untouched wilderness forest is what originally had drawn Stan and Lydia to the area. They loved the grassy Kagitwa River Valley with its low ridges backed by dramatic mountains. And they loved the enormous and ancient cedars, firs, hemlocks, and pines. Most of all they loved the idea that everything was more or less as it had been for thousands of years.

Maya had been seven months old when they had moved from the city to the ranch. They had arrived on the first day of spring. Three months later, Jake had been born. Lydia often felt that Maya's temperament reflected the tenseness of their city life, while Jake was calmer, slower moving, as though Lydia's profound happiness at being on her knees in a garden, hands patting, digging earth, had shaped Jake's temperament.

Neither Jake nor Maya had any desire to live anywhere else in the world. One or two weeks a year visiting their aunt in the city was enough for them. They loved their house, the horses, the wilderness, the freedom they had to roam the ridges.

On the return trip, Hannah and Felix pranced along the overgrown trail between the bigfoot cave and the mine camp. Maya and Jake finally let them have their heads when they reached Blue Diamond Road. They cantered to the Junction and galloped flat out to the abandoned farm, letting the wind push away thoughts and worries about Sidder's logging plans.

All that next week, Maya and Jake consumed books and articles on logging and machine maintenance. They made several trips to the library to search out the literature on sasquatch, yeti, abominable snowmen, and other extraordinary creatures whose sightings over the years humans had recorded. They found a cache of *Road Construction Gazette* and *Popular Mechanics* magazines in the used bookstore and bought all of the issues which described heavy equipment.

And every afternoon after the surveyors quit work they exercised the horses on the Blue Diamond Mine road to see what had been newly staked out. It distressed them to see that the first area to be logged lay in a direct line to the bigfoot cave. Monday loomed—the day Johnnie Stottle would begin work.

Both Maya and Jake were wide awake and watching from the front verandah when a pickup truck sped down the road, kicking up stones and dirt. After a short while Johnnie's Caterpillar groaned by the end of their lane, heading towards the abandoned farm and on up to Blue Diamond Mine.

By noon Maya and Jake were so jumpy and irritable that they argued over lunch. Lydia and Stan were surprised.

"Might do you two good to visit the Morrisons," Stan volunteered. "Sounds as though you've had enough of each other's company."

Instead, they milled around the barn, half-heartedly cleaning the loft in preparation for the new crop of hay, waiting until four o'clock when Johnnie would quit work.

They were saddled up and waiting at the abandoned farm as the pickup barreled down the mine road, rumbled across the bridge, and skidded onto the stretch of road which went by the Langhorne ranch and then curved left to meet up with the paved road to town. Johnnie had one elbow stuck out the window, one hand on the wheel. His partner, Wally Smith, was ripping a can from a six-pack of beer.

Wally Smith was a labourer Sidder hired from time to time. He couldn't drive the heavy equipment and he wasn't any good with a saw, but he always had work, driving supplies to camps, doing odd jobs. Maya and Jake knew him from the bench outside *The Kagitwa Valley Times*, where he spent his weekends. Wally never caused trouble or was rude. He just always was there, drinking cans of beer, eating slim jims and corn chips, and asking everybody who stopped whether or not it was going to rain. Maya and Jake vaguely wondered if he had a home, but never got around to asking anybody about it.

As soon as the dust had settled on the mine road, Jake and Maya galloped to the new logging camp site. Johnnie had earned his pay. He had cleared a neat rectangle and had dozed the start of a road into the bigfoot woods. The yellow earthmover was carefully parked with its back to a newly bulldozed berm of earth, a bank nearly two metres high.

By the end of the week, Johnnie had smoothed and widened the road from the spur junction to the mine. On Friday a procession of road construction and forest harvesting equipment passed the Langhornes' lane. Friday afternoon, when Jake and Maya inspected the logging camp, there were eleven machines all parked neatly with their backs to the mound of earth Johnnie had scraped from the turnaround yard. Eleven monsters were lined up, waiting for the feeding frenzy to begin when the crew arrived Monday and started their diesel stomachs churning.

"We've got to do something," Jake said.

Maya nodded her head in agreement. "You know, all week I've been thinking, 'Well, Johnnie'll make a logging camp and widen the road, but Sidder won't really come in here.' In my heart I kept hoping that they wouldn't actually start logging, that the National Park would hear about this and stop them. It's kind of like being in a dream. I mean, it was kind of an adventure to be riding up here everyday and sneaking around, scouting things out. But now I'm scared. I felt that furry little bigfoot, Jake. I really did. I held it in my arms."

"Yeah." Jake stared at the ground and kicked a clump earth of earth. "You know, when I saw all those sasquatch meeting at the stone circle, I had the oddest feeling that they were doing something they'd done forever. Like, it was a celebration—something happy. And even inside the dream I thought, they belong here and I don't. Cripes, people would think we're crazy if we told them about this stuff."

"Well," Maya straightened up in a businesslike, determined way that always made people think she was older than she was. "We saw what we saw and we know what we know. It's time for action."

"Yeah, action," Jake echoed. "This weekend we're going to have a little fun with those machines."

"A little fun with yellow Cats," Maya said. "A Cat adventure. A Cat walk."

"Yeah, and Cat stalk."

Maya and Jake began to smile as they commenced to play with words—something they had done from the time they were little.

"A doozie of a dozer adventure," Jake said. "A dozer doozie."

On his sixth birthday, Jake had laughed so hard he had fallen off his chair when Maya had made up a verse to "Dig a Hole in the Meadow." She'd just finished grade one and knew things Jake didn't. He would start school in the fall, and it was the first and only time in his life he was anxious for the summer to be over. How he longed to know all those mysterious things Maya knew. How painful it had been to watch her go to school every morning, leaving him alone.

As the family sat around singing and telling stories after the cake had been eaten and Jake had opened his presents, Jake and Maya had gotten into one of their silly moods. It was then that Maya had made up the new words to the old song.

> *The first time I saw little Jakey,*
> *He was standin' in the bathroom door*
> *Toilet paper all in his hand*
> *His underwear on the floor.*

Even Lydia and Stan had laughed until tears rolled down their cheeks. As Jake grew older and heard the story retold, he realized their amusement came not so much from the words of the song but from Jake's own hilarity—at how tickled he had been at the impromptu version. Back then just about anything that had to do with the bathroom was sure to make him laugh.

As they cantered home down the Blue Diamond Mine road, Maya and Jake made up new verses to "Dig a Hole in the Meadow," bellowing so loud they scared up birds and made the horses flatten back their ears.

The first time I saw little Sidder
He was standin' in his playhouse door
Brand new shoes all in his hand
An' his stockin' feet on the floor.

Wake up, wake up, little Sidder,
What makes you sleep so sound
The highway robbers are comin'
Gonna tear your playhouse down.

"I'll catch up to you, Jake."

Maya trotted into the trees, unzipping her jeans as she went, and ducked out of sight. Jake slowed and took the opportunity to shift his heavy pack. One of the tools had lodged in an uncomfortable position against his spine.

They had decided to leave the horses at home and go on foot on their sabotage mission. In case anything went wrong, they would not be able to be identified by Felix and Hannah's distinctive markings. There was a fork in the trail behind their place—one branch led to the high meadow and one to Smokey Boulder. The Smokey Boulder trail would bring them just below the site of the new logging camp.

At a bend in the trail Jake halted and turned to holler to Maya to hurry up.

"What're you doin' here, kid?"

Two men wearing camouflage clothing rounded the bend and blocked the trail. Jake's heart gave an enormous thud. He thought his heart would burst out of his chest. Jake peered around the men and through the trees saw the newly-scraped turn-around yard. At one end of the yard a trailer had been set up as on-site headquarters. These two must be on patrol. He did not recognize either one. Jake could smell bacon and coffee and see a make-shift table under an awning stretched from the trailer. They had just finished breakfast. Why hadn't he smelled anything earlier? Why hadn't he been more cautious?

"Uh, uh ...," Jake stuttered. His throat was too dry with fear to speak. Maya would emerge from the trees any moment now with her own pack of sabotage equipment. She had the pipe extension strapped to her backpack—they had learned that even their combined strength wasn't enough to undo the bolts where they could do the most damage. Stan had taught them the trick of using a pipe to fit over the end of a wrench to give extra leverage.

"Give me a lever and I'll lift the world." The phrase ran around in Jake's head, loud and uncontrollable. It was on his lips. He was afraid he would say it aloud. Why couldn't he think of something else to say? "Give me a lever and I'll lift the world." The longer he stood there the worse it was. They could see in his eyes what he had planned to do. They could read his mind. He had to think of something to say.

"Uh-uh .... "

One of the men adjusted a rifle slung on his shoulder. Now they were really interested. A lone kid out hiking just past dawn. A heavy pack. No need to unsling the gun, but what the heck was this kid doing here?

"Speak up, kid."

"Did ya know you were trespassing? This here's private property."

"Uh-uh .... " Again Jake stuttered.

"Hello! I didn't think we'd meet anybody on the trail." Maya popped out of the woods, smiling, using her chirpiest voice. "Don't mind my cousin, he can't talk."

Maya began to sign to Jake. She signed, "Cat. Dog. Birthday. You are my sunshine, my only sunshine. I am hungry. Where is the bathroom?" Those were all the signs she knew.

Jake flicked his fingers back at her, using his entire ASL vocabulary. "You are a weird turkey. I want a hamburger, please."

Maya turned to the men. "We're meeting our club for a camp out. This is the short cut—we didn't think anyone else knew about it."

The guards were taken aback. The signing had thrown them off. Before they could regain attention, Maya spoke again.

"You guys hunting or what? I thought deer season didn't open until the fall. Anyway, we'd better get going. We don't want to miss the rendezvous."

She moved around the men, Jake followed, wishing he were bigger so he could cover Maya's back and hide the conspicuous pipe.

They crossed the clearing, skirting the machines, and took an overgrown trail that led towards Lonesome Creek. As soon as they were out of sight of the guards they began to run. Only when they reached the protection of Smokey Boulder did they drop to the ground.

"You really are a fast thinker, Maya. That was something else."

"Not fast enough." Maya pointed to her jeans, which were wet.

They both laughed in relief.

"That was close, Jake. Now we won't be able to get to the machines any more. Sidder hired guards! When did they come up here? Those guys won't ever be too far from the machines. Did you see the trailer set-up? When did they move the trailer in?"

"Yeah. Cripes, so much for Operation Cat Stalk. And now we've got to go back the long way, with these heavy packs. Unless .... " Jake's eyes took on the almost-glazed look he got whenever he was scheming or inventing. Maya knew not to interrupt him when he was in the middle of this kind of thinking. She quietly took off her pack, unlaced and pulled off her boots, socks, and jeans. She lay the jeans to dry on a sunny patch on Smokey Boulder.

Smokey Boulder was actually a circle of boulders two metres high, with a wedge opening onto the Lonesome Creek. One of the boulders by the opening was blackened with smoke, where the few people who knew about this hideaway had built fires over the years. A stone sleeping circle protected from wind, with easy access to cool, clear water, was a gift all who knew about Smokey Boulder cherished. No one ever left any sign of habitation except for the soot on the gate stone.

Maya walked barefoot to the water's edge and stepped from rock to rock until she was in the deepest part. Then she sat and dangled her legs in the creek. Now that the rush of excitement was over, she was disappointed. Their plans—all their careful plans—were worthless. If they couldn't get close to the machines, the logging would start and the bigfeet would be driven away.

Maya thought it strange that in times of trouble she was able to think very clearly. Lydia once said she could think on her feet. But why was it that her thoughts were now so muddled? She couldn't conceive of a single way to save the bigfeet. And now she and Jake would have to go home the long way—follow the Lonesome Creek to Bird Woman Gap and then walk the railroad tracks back to the Junction.

Yes, it certainly would be too risky recrossing the logging camp area to take the shortcut home. They'd have to go the long way. The sabotage tools were heavy and would slow them down. They'd be lucky to make it home before dark, and they would have accomplished exactly nothing. The logging machines would be ready to dig into the forest tomorrow at dawn. Goodbye, wilderness. Goodbye, baby bigfoot.

In the fine sand at the base of the rock on which she sat, a claw appeared, followed by a head, another claw, and the body of a crayfish. The creature was the size of Maya's index finger and its colour matched the sand. Fascinated, Maya watched it propel itself through the water. So fast, so sleek, it moved against the current of the creek and positioned itself under another stone. Had she not been staring directly at it, she never would have seen the little crustacean.

Jake appeared at the gate stone, smiling. Maya could see he had hatched an idea.

"Camouflage," said Jake.

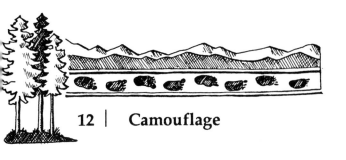

12 | Camouflage

"There are only two of them," said Jake. "The actual logging won't start until the roads are ready, right? Johnnie's got all the equipment backed up to that earth berm at the edge of the turn-around yard. Well, if we can make it across the open area to the berm, then hide behind it and move down the row, we can work on the road-building machines. That'll hold up the operation for a while. And we might even be able to drain oil from the swing machine and skidder. Then we can circle around through the woods and cross below the camp. We'll only be out in the open for a hundred metres or so. We can crawl if we have to. Once we're across the spur and the mine road we can cut through the woods and join up with the trail home. If we have to, we could stash the tools and get them later."

For the next hour Jake and Maya cut vines and small branches to camouflage their packs and clothes. By the time they reached the logging camp the sun was directly overhead. It was a fine bright day. Leaving their packs, they crept close enough to survey the clearing.

Both guards were stripped to the waist, playing cards on a makeshift table set on stretchers under an awning attached to the trailer. Already there were several empty bottles of beer on the table, and even from a distance it was easy to hear that their conversation was slow. The sun and beer were making them sleepy.

"You stayin' or what, Al? You want a hit?"

"Okay. Hit me. C'mon acey-deucey. Ouch! Another rangy jack. I'm out, Steve. I'm finished."

"They're not really patrolling," whispered Maya. "They're relaxed."

"Yeah, but look. There's the rifle."

The men laughed. The one called Al threw down his cards. Yawning, he picked up the rifle propped against the table and stepped up into the trailer.

"Gonna catch forty?"

"Yup. Nothin' else to do, except donate my money to cheaters."

The man called Steve also yawned and stretched. He swept his eyes around the wide yard and across the row of machines as he shuffled the deck of cards and lay them out for a game of solitaire.

Maya and Jake watched from the protection of the underbrush. With the noonday sun came waves of moist heat rising from the forest floor. Insects buzzed. Jays added their metallic calls to the afternoon symphony.

"Okay. Let's get to work," Jake whispered. Like crayfish in a creek, the two moved swiftly and silently back to the place where they had left their packs.

Moving stealthily, their eyes glued to the solitary guard, brother and sister stop-started around the northern perimeter of the clearing until they came to the mounded earth behind the gigantic trucks and scrapers, graders and wheel tractors. They positioned themselves just over the berm from a D7H Caterpillar like the one that Johnnie had used during the Morrison fire, and crawled to the berm crest to watch Steve the guard. On their bellies, using elbows and knees to pull and push themselves forward, they slithered into the open and down to the protection of the tractor. There was plenty of room to move underneath the machine and the shade was welcome. Both were sweating and thirsty from eating so much dust.

From under the Cat they had a false sense of security. If Steve had been looking, he would have seen them, although his eyes may have mistaken their forms for shadows.

Silently, quickly, they found the proper wrench to remove the tractor's oil drain plug. The model was exactly like one they had read about. The plug was coated with dust and grease, but budged with only the use of a wrench. Jake kept watch while Maya worked the plug loose. She moved an arm's length away for the last two turnings, but still got splashed by the rush of oil draining from the huge machine. And when she replaced the plug, she could feel her clothes soaking up oil from the drenched earth underneath the oil pan.

Draining oil from the second, third, and fourth machines went smoothly. The fifth machine, however, was not so easily conquered. Jake had to slide the length of pipe over the wrench handle, and it took the two of them to loosen the nut. The oil spurted out, splattering both of them. And when Jake pulled the pipe from the wrench so Maya could replace the nut, it clanked against the undercarriage of the machine.

They froze. All the surrounding sounds of bird and breeze and insect also seemed suddenly to stop, creating a lull in which the slightest stirring could be heard. Maya's breathing seemed a roar to Jake, and his breath as rasping as a sprinter's to Maya.

The card player cleared his throat. There was a clink, the sound of a bottle brushing another, then silence. The moments stretched out. At last came the rhythmic sound of cards being slapped down. Maya and Jake exchanged looks. They wouldn't tempt fate by doing another machine. It was time to go.

Easing from underneath the yellow monster, brother and sister crawled up and over the berm. They retreated behind the berm, rewrapped the tools and adjusted their camouflage foliage. They made their way through the forest, crossed the tracks, road, and open space without a hitch, and soon were well on their way back home.

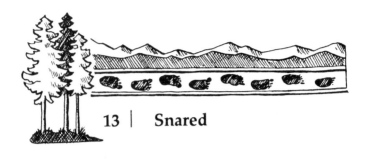

13 | Snared

"We need a long-term plan, Jake."

Maya and Jake sat on the bench outside *The Kagitwa Valley Times*, waiting for Lydia to finish work. Sometimes she liked to spend a Saturday evening doing the books, and often Maya and Jake would accompany her and go to the movies. It was the one night of the week when there was a little excitement in town. Since they had seen the only movie playing at the Palace the night after the Morrison fire, they just poked around town.

"Yeah, I guess this is bigger than the two of us. And I don't feel so hot about about what we did. We broke the law, you know. Monday morning when Johnnie and the crew discover what we did to the machines we could be in big trouble."

"Hiya kids."

"Hi, Eliot."

"Lydia said to tell you she's got another half hour's work and for you to see if there are any canning jars at the Miracle Mart."

Like Lydia, Eliot Thompson was from the east. He had done well in publishing, retired early, and had realized a lifelong dream of running a small newspaper. He had brought his city desktop publishing know-how and plunked himself down in the Kagitwa Valley and stayed. He was editor, reporter, and printer. *The Kagitwa Valley Times* competed with *The South Valley Herald* and the Coast City dailies, but slowly readers had turned to Eliot's weekly paper. Now, after ten years, *The Kagitwa Valley Times* had a substantial and faithful readership.

"The mountains are crawling with ex-city-slickers," Eliot had told Lydia soon after the paper started up. Eliot had met the Langhornes and liked them right off. When he found out about Lydia's work experience, he pestered her until she agreed to work part-time with him. "Yes, ex-slickers and folks who are starved for a good laugh, a good whack of local news, and somebody who is financially independent enough to speak the truth."

Eliot had regular battles with Sidder & Company and other logging operators, with people who wanted to dam the Kagitwa River, with ski resort developers who wanted this or that. Eliot kept an attorney in nearly constant employ. "It's all part of the fun," he would say.

Eliot had hired help to get advertizing and to distribute papers that didn't go with the mail run, and had hired Lydia to do his bookkeeping and to advise him on financial matters. Lydia liked keeping her hand in a business—she had always been an astute planner and accountant. She and Eliot worked well together, and the money was good. With what she earned and what Stan made from outside carpentry jobs, the family had economic security. And Lydia especially liked being able to set her own hours, though she mostly worked midweek afternoons.

"So, what are you two schemers up to this summer? How's Hard-hearted Hannah?"

Maya and Jake smiled. Eliot had never been comfortable around horses. Once when he had come for supper, they insisted that he have a ride on Hannah. The ordinarily sweet, docile dappled grey had taken the bit in her teeth the moment Eliot had mounted and had galloped around the pasture as though there were a burdock under her girth. Eliot hung on, but barely, and was only too happy to slide to the ground when Hannah calmed to a trot and finally walked innocently back to the fence, where the Langhornes were splitting themselves with laughter. The image of Eliot flopping all over the saddle was one which never failed to amuse them.

"Eliot, did you know that Sidder's really going to log the Blue Diamond land? Johnnie's cleared a camp and they moved in the heavy equipment on Friday."

"Yeah, and did you know," Jake added, "that they've got a road started from the mine back towards the high field behind our place."

Maya was afraid Jake would give away too much information. She did not want Eliot to ask about their trips to the camp. She piled on another question.

"And do you think Sidder is really interested in just that little square of forest?"

Eliot studied the serious faces of the children. Maya's startlingly green eyes were close-set, like Lydia's. Jake's eyes had Lydia's dark blue, but were wide-set, like Stan's. Both had thick mops of light brown hair. Until this summer they had been about the same height. Now Maya was stretching out. They still dressed like twins, in jeans and tee-shirts. Maya wore the Australian hat Eliot had given her several years before on her birthday, and Jake had on his gen-u-ine Stetson.

Sometimes when Eliot looked at the Langhorne kids he became lost in an admiration tinged with sadness. How different they were from his own children. These kids were independent, reliable, and loving. Their family worked together and really seemed to enjoy one another's company. Eliot had pangs of remorse for the way his own family life had been. He had barely seen his children. For years his focus had been on work. All of a sudden he was attending high school and college graduations. All of a sudden, it seemed, the children were grown and gone. He rarely heard from them now, barely knew them. And his wife, well, that was another sadness. He guessed that he barely knew her, either. She was still living in the east and had remarried. The children visited her all the time.

"Who owns the forest on the east side of the Kagitwa? Is it Sidder's land?"

"Well, kids, here's the scoop. Sidder's lawyer boys have their fingers through a loophole in the covenant. They figure they can get authorization from the government to clearcut that whole area—both the Diamond Mine tract and the east side of the Kagitwa. Sidder's been buying up private land over there under different company names. He owns another thousand hectares of land just opposite the Blue Diamond tract. Looks like an open book on the map. Likely he'll build a bridge over the Kagitwa at the Junction narrows and haul timber out that way, out past your place.

"Meanwhile, I guess they'll strip or selection cut the forest in back of your place. Or at least pretend to."

Eliot noted the distress which registered on both children's faces. *They look so old—so worried,* he was thinking. *They really care. My kids couldn't have cared less if the entire country had been clearcut.*

"There's a meeting tomorrow night. Some locals and the native group. And a lawyer who worked on the Tsitika Valley preservation project—Sarah Tallwood—is coming. Tallwood was able to get an interim order to stop logging up there until the land issue was settled."

"Can we come?" Maya asked.

"Can we come?" Jake echoed.

Eliot smiled at their parroting. "You can come, you can come," he said. "It starts at eight, in the Little School."

Sunday night the Langhornes and Morrisons drove to town together. Sam, Karen, Maya, and Jake rode in the back of the pickup.

Jake wagged his finger at the four adults squeezed into the cab. "You're breaking the law!"

Nina, who was sitting on Alec's lap, laughed and pointed to the seat belt, which was stretched across the two of them.

"We buckled up, so just you mind your own business, youngster."

At the town bridge the four back passengers jumped out.

"See you oldsters later," Jake called. "Save us seats!"

Karen treated everybody to pop at the Miracle Mart. Just as they were taking first gulps, in came one of the logging camp guards.

"Thought you two was campin' out."

Jake spritzed a mouthful of pop, wetting the front of his shirt and getting some on the guard. Maya nearly did the same, but caught herself in time. Sam choked on his own drink, sputtered and began to laugh uncontrollably. Any social gaff made Sam hysterical, especially one which contained a burp or fart or slopped food. Karen went rapid-fire through a succession of reactions: surprise, amusement, embarrassment, and finally curiosity.

"You two were camping?" she asked. "Jake— did you guys camp out without us? When?"

Jake wanted the floor to open and swallow him. If he spoke, he would blow the lie Maya had told the men. If he didn't speak, Karen would push him and it would be obvious to the guard that she expected an answer, in other words, that he could talk.

"Uh-uh," Jake stuttered, pop trickling down his chin. He futilely brushed drops of sticky cola from his front and looked at the damage he had done to the guard's shirt. "Uh-uh .... "

Jake stared at Maya, begging her to think of some way out of this mess.

"Uh .... "

"He's choking," Maya said, and before another sound could come from Jake's lips, Maya whacked him on the back with all her strength.

"You're disgusting!" Maya gave him a rough push, making him stumble forward. "We can dress you up, but we sure can't take you out. Where'd you learn to drink from a bottle? In a barn with a runt pig?" All the while she was talking, she was moving Jake towards the door with her free hand. "Good thing you can't hear yourself, you pig."

Outside, Maya made a pretense of signing to Jake. Since one hand was holding the bottle of pop, it looked like a bizarre comedy—Maya alternately flicking her fingers and pushing Jake along the sidewalk. Karen and Sam hurried after them, snorting in their efforts to suppress laughter. Bewildered, the guard watched the little procession from inside the Miracle Mart. He made no move to follow. "Idiot kids," he muttered as he grabbed two six-packs of cola from the cooler and dug into his jeans for money. "Bunch of morons in this valley."

At the corner, Maya turned back to watch the guard leave the store and get into his pickup. He must have left his partner back at the logging camp and made this Sunday night beverage run to town. Steve, that was his name. The other one was called Al. Maya's heart raced and for the first time real fear entered her bones about the magnitude of their sabotage actions.

Still chortling in admiration for his friend, Sam punched Jake in the arm. "Hey, did you two really go camping?"

Maya looked at her watch. "Naw, we were just scouting for our overnighter with the horses," she said. "Come on, it's eight o'clock. We'd better run."

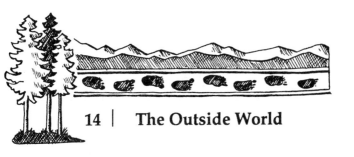

14 | The Outside World

The Little School, as it was called much to the chagrin of fifth and sixth graders who no longer considered themselves little, was built overlooking the Kagitwa River in the early 1900s. The playground had been fenced to keep young students away from the river's steep banks and swift currents.

The high school—Kagitwa Valley Junior and Senior High—had been built in the 1960s opposite the Little School, and was a long two-storey building to which students from the entire valley were bussed.

In the fall, Maya and Karen would be in grade seven and would be moving across the road. Though it was physically not far, the move marked an immense transition and distance from childish ways. Jake hated the idea of being left behind. But that was a long way off. And there were other matters of concern at the moment.

The library of the Little School was packed with an odd assortment of people. Maya and

Jake spotted some of their teachers, many of the storekeepers, neighbours from along the town road, and parents of school friends. Johnnie Stottle was there, cap on tight, sitting between Wally Smith and a woman who seemed uncomfortable in crowds. Some people were obviously from the city, dressed up and stiff, and others looked like leftovers from hippie times, except that they could not possibly be more than eighteen or twenty years old. There were weathered and shy pairs who seldom left their mountain retreats and people from the local native council and natives from the larger coast councils. Ski resort owners and other seasonal residents formed an identifiable cluster in chairs by the windows, their expensive clothing signalling their wealth.

Nina Morrison was speaking as the Langhorne and Morrison kids took seats by their parents.

"And so we invited Mr. Sidder to come to this meeting, but I see he isn't here. Is there someone representing him?" Silence followed. Eyes roved the room. A few people focused on a remarkably clean-shaven and tanned man in a back corner. The man caught the attention, imperceptibly shifted in his seat, and then scanned the room, as though he, too, were looking for a Sidder & Company representative.

Maya gave Jake an elbow and lifted an eyebrow. Jake nodded in agreement.

"The native council and a group of us local residents got together. We thought we needed this meeting to discuss the logging plans for Blue Diamond Mine tract and for the forestland opposite it across the Kagitwa River."

Nina Morrison was a natural spokesperson, a woman everyone seemed to like and respect. She was known both for her warmth and for her ability to size up situations quickly and organize people to appropriate action.

"What we need to do tonight is get information out and hear everybody's point of view. We're not all tree huggers and spotted owl fanatics. We're here because we live in this valley together and need to talk about what's going on.

"The Blue Diamond Mine land is one of the last remnants of the ancient western wildwood. The hemlock, Sitka spruce, western red cedar, Douglas fir, and Pacific silver fir that grow in our valley are valuable to Mr. Sidder for timber, of course. We understand that. But the land is the watershed for the whole valley. All our drinking water, all our ground water depends on those slopes. Clearcutting would mean slides. Houses and farms at the foot of clearcut mountains would be worthless.

And the Kagitwa River would get silted up. The whole valley environment would be changed. We know the heartbreak some of the folks who live in Rainbow Valley went through two years ago. A lifetime of work to build a place and whoosh—the first heavy rain and down comes the mountain mud to cover the valley and clog the river.

"Now, the National Park made an offer to buy the land and Mr. Sidder refused that offer. We have learned that Mr. Sidder has been buying up the forest north of here, land opposite the Blue Diamond tract. Some of us have been talking about setting up a land fund to see if we can raise enough money to help the National Park buy both pieces of land. But that's just an idea. We're here tonight to find out everybody's point of view. Guess that's all I have to say for the moment."

Karen and Sam squirmed in their seats and halfway through their mother's speech had begun to whisper. They had tried to engage their friends in covert conversation, but both Maya and Jake listened intently to Nina, drinking up every word. A warm feeling began to infuse them as they realized they were not alone in wanting to protect the forest. They sensed a similar passion to their own among some of those gathered in the room, and yet these people knew nothing about the bigfeet.

As the evening wore on, the reality of dream-flight excursions faded and the importance of saving mythical sasquatch shifted to protecting the Kagitwa watershed and keeping their own downslope home from being washed away.

One of the men who worked with Johnnie Stottle rose to speak. "First of all, we're not going to clearcut in there. We're mostly selection cutting, just the good ripe timber that otherwise would fall over and ruin the forest. We'll be replanting any strip cuts after we harvest, and leaving the forest in better shape than we found it."

Ida Jones, owner of the Miracle Mart, was next to speak. "Bob Sidder has done more for this county than maybe anybody else in this room. He hires locally, does business with us, brings a lot of side employment to the town. And you know our rink would never have been built if it hadn't been for Mr. Sidder's generous donation."

The emotions in the room began to run high. There was a polarization that Maya and Jake registered in their chests—they felt scared or excited or both. Never before had they been part of such an affair. Karen and Sam, bored, had left the meeting to hang out in the parking lot with other friends who had lost interest in the proceedings.

After each speaker, Nina Morrison rose, and like a wave of calm her voice smoothed the surface of the crowd. She thanked each person sincerely and found a point of agreement, no matter how trivial, and reiterated it before calling on the next speaker. When it seemed that everyone had said everything, a native woman rose from a side seat and began to talk in a low voice.

"The land we live on is not to be bought and sold. The forest is not to be harvested like a field of corn. A mountain stripped of trees and replanted in straight rows is not a healthy mountain.

"The land claimed by Mr. Sidder's company and before that by the Blue Diamond Mine Company was never given to them by the people who have lived here for thousands of years. The land which Mr. Sidder wishes to log is sacred to us. It is a place of great spiritual meaning to native people. That is all I wish to say. Thank you."

No one spoke for a long moment after the woman sat down. Maya and Jake heard a whispered, "That's Sarah Tallwood—the lawyer from Tsitika Valley."

Nina slowly rose to her feet. "Well, thank you all for coming tonight, and I hope any of you who are interested in setting up a Land Fund will come to our ranch next Saturday night at eight .... " Someone at the back of the room caught her attention. "Would you like to say something, Mrs. Stottle?"

All eyes turned to the wrinkled and worn woman who got to her feet with the help of a cane and Johnnie's strong hands on her elbow and back. She had on a much-repaired sweater with a cheap ornament pinned to it. Maya and Jake had never seen her before although they knew about her, knew Johnnie lived with her in the old Stottle place and supported her. She had taken care to dress up for the meeting. She had on a little hat, stuck to her head with a fancy old-fashioned hatpin, and her dress had a lace collar attached to it with a brooch. Around her neck was a chain which held a watch and a smooth gold wedding ring, now too small to fit her work-enlarged fingers.

"I ain't much for public speaking," Mrs. Stottle said. She gave a nervous, self-conscious laugh and the room grew even more unbearably quiet. "I been in the Valley all my life," Mrs. Stottle went bravely on. Johnnie had his head down, his arms between his legs. He looked like a schoolboy.

"My daddy was a logger and my mama cooked at camps. We was all born in camps. And I met my husband right here and he was a logger too. We got ourselves a piece of land and the timber off it fed us and our kids. Now,

I got eight kids, and none of 'em would have had nothin' if it hadn't been for loggin'. Them trees paid for food and clothes and education. My Johnnie, he's the only one stayed in the Valley and been workin' at the woods. The rest is gone. They got good jobs and nice families, too. My Johnnie looks after me real good. And Mr. Sidder give him a fine job now, and Johnnie's gonna be able to buy himself a nice double-wide and fix himself up a place of his own. He's got a little spot picked out on the land. And that's what I want to say to you people tonight. That land grows trees real fast. You can cut 'em down and new ones'll grow up. There's plenty of woods. Mr. Sidder can't even make a dint in the woods, so I don't think we should be interferin' with his business."

Mrs. Stottle sat down. Johnnie looked up for a minute, as though he, too, were going to say something, and then adjusted his cap. Nina thanked Mrs. Stottle, asked if anyone else had anything to say, and ended the meeting.

People lingered on the Little School steps and in the high school parking lot across the road to discuss what had been said. Maya and Jake felt stunned. Mixed with the near-euphoria of discovering how many others shared the desire to save the woods was a realization that Mrs. Stottle and others also had points of view which made sense. And what had started as a gnawing uneasiness about their sabotage of Sidder's machines grew into full-fledged fear and terror of being caught. The guards could identify them—that was obvious. Had they covered their tracks well enough? Would their parents find out about Saturday's secret sabotage mission? The burden of what they had done weighed more heavily on them than anything they had ever done in their lives. What would Monday morning bring?

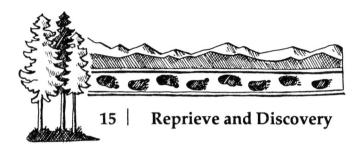

Dream-flying and bigfeet were the furthest things from Jake and Maya's minds that night as they sat on Jake's bed and worried over the sabotage. They mentally traced and retraced their steps, agonizing about whether or not there might be tracks which would give them away. As they went through all the possibilities and what-ifs, a growing sense of doom brought their spirits lower and lower. If they were caught, Stan and Lydia would be shocked and disappointed beyond words. Trust was a big thing with the Langhorne family. Lydia and Stan trusted them and had always trusted them. The few times when something bordered on a breach of trust, the situation was discussed in detail and explained. Breaking trust was the worst possible offense in their family.

The sabotage had the potential of doing even further harm to the family. What if they had to pay for the damage? What would their neighbours and friends think? Eliot wouldn't want to keep Lydia at the paper, not when the story of her outlaw kids was splashed across the front page of *The Kagitwa Valley Times*.

And what did they have to say in their own defense? That they had seen sasquatch in their dreams and wanted to save them from Sidder's logging operation? The more they developed the scenario, the more they thought about the consequences of their actions, the more desperate they grew.

"Maybe we should tell Ma and Pop what we did," Maya sighed. She felt beyond tears. This was a whole new landscape of emotion, and she did not like the look of it one bit. It was not anything like all the new stuff that had happened this year when her period had started and her body had begun to change. That had been unknown territory, too, but exciting, like an adventure. This was horrid and scary.

"Yeah, maybe we should." Jake punched his pillow into shape and pulled his quilt up over his ears. "Goodnight, Maya. I'm sorry."

"Me, too, Jake. I'm older, I should have thought it through more."

Even in such dire straits Jake's sensitivity about their age surfaced. "Not that much older. I should have known better too."

Maya returned to her room and lay in bed, unable to sleep. After a while she went downstairs and made herself a cup of cocoa. "I must be growing up," she thought. "There's nobody to blame except myself."

***

"You two look wiped." Lydia had come in from the garden, her face smudged and her nails dark with earth. "Have some strawberries."

Stan came in from staking out the ground on the south side of the kitchen.

"We're ready to dig!"

Stan's enthusiasm had carried them through some very arduous projects. He was a careful planner and a cheerful worker. For the most part Maya and Jake enjoyed working with him. He liked to sing and had a rich tenor voice. He knew the words to hundreds of songs.

Stan noted Maya and Jake's lack of enthusiasm for digging the foundation for the kitchen addition, but made no comment.

The phone rang. Maya and Jake froze. Inside, each had a sinking feeling. This was it. Johnnie Stottle would have been at work exactly one hour by now. He would have discovered their sabotage and have had time to drive to town and phone Sidder. They knew they wouldn't lie if Lydia confronted them. Yes, this was it.

They watched Lydia's face for clues as she listened to the speaker on the other end. The clock ticked loudly but the hands seemed to have stopped dead. Little beads of sweat appeared on Jake's forehead and Maya's hands went cold.

"Isn't that great," Lydia said at last. "That's just great. Thanks for calling. Bye now."

Maya and Jake collapsed inwardly. Their faces, a moment before drained of blood, flushed red.

"Eliot just heard that Sidder's delaying the logging operation until he has a chance to talk with us. He wants a spokesperson for the native council and for the local residents to meet him next Monday to discuss his Blue Diamond plans. Now isn't that a first!"

Maya and Jake's spirits flew. The morning opened up. They joked and babbled through breakfast. Afterwards they joyfully grabbed spades and dug with great gusto.

"If YOU go down to the WOODS today, you'd BET-ter not go aLONE." Stan sang "The Teddy Bears' Picnic" as he dug through the grassy turf. He paced himself and the tempo of the song to match his work.

It's lovely down in the woods today,
But safer to stay at home
For every bear that ever there was

*Will gather there for certain because
Today's the day that teddy bears have
    their picnic.*

Jake and Maya found themselves digging in the same rhythm—stepping on the spades, plunging them into the earth, angling back on the handles to loosen the clods, then lifting and throwing each spadeful in time with the song.

One song led to another. Stan had a way of judging their fatigue and called for rests just before they were too tired. Soon they had dug away a neat rectangle of matted grass and were ready to begin digging to the final depth. Then Stan would build forms and they would mix, pour, and smooth a concrete foundation pad.

As they began to dig the second layer, Jake reprised the first song, setting a faster tempo. "For EV'ry BEAR that EVer there WAS will GAther THERE for CERtain beCAUSE .... " Jake stopped midsong and his jaw dropped open.

"That's IT!" he exclaimed. "That's IT! That's what they were doing!"

"What?" Stan and Maya asked in unison.

Jake came back to the present. "Uh, just, uh. Just a dream I had, that's all. It just came back to me."

Stan took up the song again and resumed digging. Maya wanted to ask more questions, but resisted and also turned back to work.

"SEE them gaily GAD about, they love to PLAY and shout they NEVER have any CARES ... "

Maya screeched and fell on her knees. She sifted through the earth to uncover an object and held it up.

"I KNEW it! I knew I'd find one. I just knew one of these days I'd find one and today is the day. Oh, lookie lookie look!"

Maya held a bone arrowhead in the palm of her hand.

The rest of the foundation area was dug with more enthusiasm than Stan had ever seen brought to such a task. He joked that maybe they should start on the new barn foundation while everyone was so excited about excavating.

Later, Maya asked Jake what he had discovered when they were digging.

"Remember the dream I told you about? With all those different kinds of sasquatch meeting at the stone circle? Well, it's exactly like the song—I mean, when I was little and Pop first sang that song, I could see teddy bears walking and talking and having a picnic down in some green place by a stream. And that's what the sasquatch were doing in my dream. They were having a bigfoot picnic!"

That night, Maya fell asleep clutching her arrowhead and Jake drifted happily into dreamland clutching the image of his own wonderful discovery. And in their dreams they travelled to a place near Narnauk Peak. Unlike the previous time when they had missed each other in dream flight, they met that night at a stone circle where a great many beings were gathered.

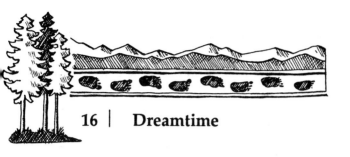

Plump huckleberries weighted tall bushes. Rabbit and squirrel, cougar, black bear, and wolf appeared and disappeared in the endless and changing theatre. Yellow jackets added to a happy chorus of birds flitting from a stream to a fringe of red alder and vine maple, sometimes darting into the green gloom of the ancient evergreen forest, where massive hemlocks, cedars, firs and spruces stood like giants. Sword fern, deer fern, lady fern— countless species of plants grew from a carpet of moss below the umbrellas of the giants. Foam flowers, violets and the red of ten thousand bunchberries dotted the green carpet with colour. A nurse log, covered by sprouting hemlock babies, lay in a swath of sunlight, the only break in the canopy of conifers.

Black-maned elk and black-tailed deer migrated the steep trails which crisscrossed the forest, leading across spawning streams of steelhead and salmon to the high, cool meadows of summer.

A ridge of sitting trees marked the south end of a sunny meadow. Blue-eyed grasses, blue lupines, and fire-red paintbrush bloomed in the tall grasses. The sitting trees were on a downhill slope of the meadow. Their trunks grew horizontal to the ground for a short span before curving up and straight to the sky like other cedars and firs. When the trees had been young, the weight of winter snows had bent them downhill.

A configuration of smooth glacial rocks by the sitting trees looked for all the world like a meeting place, a circle for dancing, or a natural setting for a campfire. Beyond the circle of stone, forming the east border of the meadow, was a series of caves with scraggly and crooked trees growing up between the rocks. Some of the stunted trees, twisted by wind and heavy snows, looked like thin bodies of dancers frozen in position. Some of the cave entrances were partly hidden by these dwarf trees.

Here and there on the higher slopes above the rock caves were patches of snowbanks, shaded from the midsummer sun by mountain summits behind them.

Jake straddled one of the sitting trees and sucked on a shaft of sweet grass. Before him, their faces stained with wild strawberry and huckleberry juice, young sasquatch wrestled and tumbled in the grassy centre of the stone circle. Baby bigfeet imitated their older siblings, rolling head over heels or jumping on top of other sprawled youngsters.

Jake watched many other creatures move among the shadows in the woods below the sitting tree ridge. There were tiny horses, no bigger than cats, and enormous birds which lurched and jumped to landings in open patches of the forest created by blowdowns. This was the season of plenty. It seemed to Jake that there had been a truce called on this day between hunter and hunted, for below him young foxes romped and rolled with their mother, making no effort to stalk a partridge hen and her chicks who scurried and pecked nearby. And baby elks lay sunning in grass nests as their herd grazed the high meadow, undisturbed by mountain panthers languidly napping no more than a lunge away.

As the afternoon drew to a close, the sasquatch gathered in the stone circle. Young and old, some huge, some bear-sized, red-haired, black-haired, and a few white-haired, the bigfeet lounged in the now beaten-down grass of the inner circle. There was a sense of contentment as they lay around, bellies plump from the berry feast.

Jake settled comfortably against the natural backrest of fragrant cedar bark and watched the happy scene before him. The sun set, and in the lavender afterglow of day, a crescent moon appeared. Beside it, one by one, three bright planets came out, forming a backwards L tipped on its back, the short arm closest to the slender backwards C of new moon.

Movement from the direction of the rock caves drew Jake's attention. Quietly and almost as if in slow motion, a line of humans made their way to the circle. Some of them wore capes of woven goat hair and the soft inner bark of cedar. Others were painted. Each one, from the littlest toddler to the most sedate elder, bore a gift—a carved wooden bowl filled with the sweetest berries, a woven tray of ground acorn cakes, a stick skewered with choice pieces of dried salmon. All these gifts were placed at the center of the circle. And then the givers took seats on the smooth surrounding boulders.

Maya was among the young people. Around her neck was an elkhorn amulet and her hair was held by a wooden comb carved in the shape of a bear holding a fish on its knees. Maya came to sit by Jake, and the other young adults also took places nearby Jake on the sitting trunks. And it seemed as though elk and deer, wolves and cougars, animals large and small, had also moved in, making concentric rings around the stone circle.

No one spoke a word or uttered a sound. Bigfoot and human babies nestled sleepily in the arms of their parents. All sat in silent harmony as the midsummer's light faded from the sky and the configuration of moon and planets moved slowly eastward. The only sounds were of meadow frogs and night insects chirruping, fiddling, peeping their summer songs to the stars.

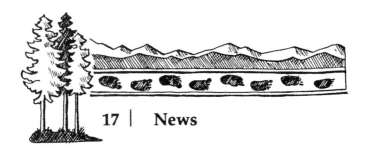

17 | News

Tuesday morning Maya and Jake awoke refreshed, though their muscles were sore from digging. They moved slowly, dreamily through the morning chores, and it was not until they sat down to breakfast that both realized with a start that the morning could bring news of their sabotage. They listened intently to the radio, and sighed with relief when no mention was made of logging camp vandalism.

Neither Maya nor Jake had ever taken much interest in newspapers, except for the comics. If their family had had a television, news likely would have been the last thing they would have watched. They sometimes found their parents' radio listening habits annoying—the programs were either morning or afternoon interview shows or news specials. Sunday was especially dreadful—from nine in the morning until noon Lydia and Stan found inside chores to do so that they could listen to a long news program that drove Maya and Jake nuts.

The only time the living room radio could be tuned to any decent music was Saturday night, so Maya and Jake had saved and bought small portable radios and often listened to rock and roll far into the night. When Maya and Jake had been younger, Lydia or Stan would creep into their rooms when they were asleep to turn off and remove the radios from under their pillows. Now that Maya and Jake were older, Lydia and Stan respected their right to privacy and, unless the music bled through pillows and walls, nothing was said about late-night listening.

Wednesday morning they both trotted to the mailbox at the end of their lane to fetch *The Kagitwa Valley Times*. They scanned the front page, fear of discovery knotting their guts.

And there was the bold headline:

LOGGING OPERATION STOPPED?
After a meeting of Kagitwa Valley residents on Sunday evening, a representative of Robert S. Sidder & Company contacted the leaders of a local action group and a local native group to suggest further discussion. For the meantime, the planned logging of Blue Diamond Mine area has been postponed.

There were lengthy quotes from various speakers at Sunday's meeting and a summary of the history of the National Park's negotiations with Sidder & Company, as well as a reprint of the covenant which had protected the land from the time of its sale by Blue Diamond Mine. The woman who had spoken so quietly and powerfully near the end of the meeting, Sarah Tallwood, had decided to work as legal counsel for the local native group.

Eliot devoted his weekly editorial to the logging issue, and in his usual bold manner raised a number of questions pertaining to the mudslides which had ruined several homes downslope from a clearcut section of Sidder's land in Rainbow Valley. There were five letters to the editor, four of which spoke about economic and social benefits of logging to the Kagitwa Valley.

Without realizing it, Maya and Jake had stopped and sat on the bridge wall as they read the paper, one hanging onto the left page, the other onto the right, both heads buried as they took turns reading aloud.

"Yoo-hoo! Maya! Jake!" Lydia stood on the front verandah and waved. Lydia and Stan both enjoyed leisurely breakfasts and especially liked to linger over the newspaper with second cups of coffee.

Wednesday afternoon Maya and Jake decided to ride up to the logging camp to see what was going on.

"Do you realize we're returning to the scene of the crime," Maya said as they saddled the horses. "Just like real criminals do."

"We're just exercising horses on a public access road," Jake said. "We won't go too close—not close enough for Al and Steve to recognize us as the hikers. We'll just see if there's anything new."

They cantered Hannah and Felix from the abandoned farm to the Junction and slowed to a wary walk as they moved towards the logging camp. From a distance it was clear that the guards were indeed still living in the camp trailer headquarters. Maya and Jake heard gunshots. Out of boredom, the men must be target practicing, and so brother and sister turned their horses towards home without going close enough to see the yellow earthmovers lined up and waiting for action.

For the next few days their hearts thudded in fear as they listened to the morning news. With each new day came a further realization of the weight of their sabotage acts. Like mice stunned and frozen by the stare of a cat which has cornered them, Maya and Jake were unable to talk about what they had done and unable to think of any solutions. So deadened were they by their own actions that they spent hours doing nothing, eyes glazed and thoughts paralyzed.

Saturday night a group of Valley residents gathered at the Morrisons'. Should Sidder decide to sell the land to the National Park, they knew he would be determined to get an equivalent amount of money that the timber would bring. They also knew the politics of the park system and that the park was firm in its final offer. That left Kagitwa Valley residents to use their ingenuity to raise any additional amount demanded by Sidder. Plans were laid for a land fund. They named it the Kagitwa Watershed Protection Fund and decided to hold a benefit barbecue and concert the following weekend.

The main concern of those gathered at the Morrisons' was to get support from the entire community. Those whose livelihoods depended on the forest industry and those who believed that reforestation was good stewardship of the land must agree with the aims of the Land Fund. Splitting the community over such an issue could be worse than Sidder's clearcutting the mountain. Even mud slides could be cleaned up, but bad blood among neighbours flowed for many generations.

Aside from two babies-in-arms, Maya and Jake were the only young people who stayed through the entire meeting. Karen, Sam, and friends had gone off to the workshop loft with a boom box, several bowlfuls of popcorn, and a plate piled high with chocolate chip cookies.

"It's a matter of education," Nina said. "All of us here are fairly romantic about nature. Maybe we're unrealistic. Maybe there are companies who are helping the forest in the long run with their logging. We should do some research ourselves. And then we can present the bad practices alongside the good ones—be balanced, in other words. Sidder obviously made a mistake at Rainbow Valley, and that's to our advantage because it buys us time. When we meet with him tomorrow we'll see if we can bargain for time while Sarah Tallwood works on the native land claim aspect. Meanwhile, we've got two things in motion— build up the Land Fund and educate ourselves and the Valley about logging."

Eliot looked around the Morrison kitchen at his friends. A few more layers of his city cynicism fell away. He loved these people. For the first time in his life he had a sense of family.

"Information is my game," Eliot said. "The newspaper is at your service."

As they listened to the discussion, Jake and Maya felt more and more numbed by the complexity of the adult world. When Nina summarized the problem, it seemed simple, yet when she stopped talking, the complexity flooded back. The torment over imminent discovery mixed with their growing confusion about what was right or wrong about logging and what they should do to save the home of the bigfeet, whether or not bigfeet were real.

When Nina said what was needed was education, Maya and Jake had the same image of schoolrooms filled with dead air and hard chairs, endless hours of sitting punctuated by occasional bursts of energy when a particular subject actually held their interest enough to make them forget that they were confined inside, forbidden to come and go at will, not even allowed to take care of basic needs, such as using the toilet or getting a drink of water. Education. What did Nina mean?

The formal part of the meeting ended. Fiona Lynch took her fiddle from its case and tuned it. Someone got a mandolin and someone else a guitar. Stan began to sing a round in his melodious tenor as the musicians were tuning, and Alec and Nina set out mugs of coffee and plates of homemade sweets.

Noticing Jake and Maya alone in a corner, Lydia crossed the room and put her arms around them.

"Why so serious?" she asked.

"Ma, what does Nina mean about education?" Maya felt helpless and on the brink of tears. "Do you think that people like Mrs. Stottle will ever change their minds? I mean, why can't people just leave things alone? Why can't we have a forest that maybe nobody ever does anything with. Just let it be there in case there are creatures in it who need to be safe from humans?"

"Yeah," Jake said. He leaned against Lydia the way he used to when he was little and needed to climb into her lap and cry about something. "What if there are creatures living in there that need privacy? Creatures that will die or be trapped and caged if they are found?"

Lydia looked into the faces of these two who sometimes in the oddest moments appeared as strangers to her. What rich interior lives they have, she was thinking. How glad I am we moved out here. Like the strings of Fiona's violin, Lydia felt an almost physical vibration in sympathy with Maya and Jake. She remembered a similar wistfulness or sadness of her own. Images of her childhood floated to the surface. In the city, where she had spent her entire life until the move to Kagitwa Valley, there was an old birch tree in a park, set off by itself from the main playground. The birch had soft long grass growing between its roots. It was there Lydia would retreat to read and think. It was there that she had dreamed up the wilderness and only later had found it again in books. Her first impression when she and Stan had travelled to the Kagitwa Valley was one of coming to a place she already had seen in dreams.

"Do you believe in spirits, Ma?" Jake asked. "Or like, uh, sasquatch and bigfeet and stuff like that?"

"I used to think a birch tree was my best friend and that at night after I left my secret hiding place, beings who lived down under the roots would play in the grass where I'd sat. Sometimes they left little messages for me, like sticks crossed just so, or a piece of green eggshell with a tiny flower in it. Does that answer your question?"

"Ma," Maya's eyes were brimming with tears. "There's no answer to anything. Mrs. Stottle wouldn't have a home if Johnnie lost his job with Mr. Sidder. Without the logging industry, the town would be poor—even Eliot's newspaper would fold, I bet. Maybe all those trees are going to die soon, the way that biologist said, and maybe lightning will strike and fire will burn everything anyway. If even nice people can't agree about something like this ... oh, I don't know ... everything is so ... so complicated and messed up."

Lydia wanted to comfort Maya, but she recognized how accurate Maya's assessment was of the whole mess humans had gotten themselves into. "You're way ahead of most of the adults I've ever known, Maya. You, too, Jake. I can't tell you what a thrill it is for me to hear you talk this way. I wish I had an answer for you."

Stan lowered himself onto the floor, balancing a tray on which were glasses of lemonade and an assortment of cookies. "The mountain comes to Mohammed," he said.

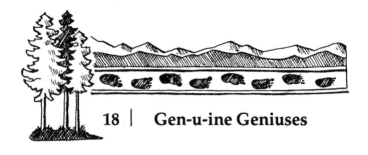

"Can I come in, Maya?"

"Sure."

Maya sat at her table, idly drawing. Jake flopped on her bed and stared at the ceiling. For a while neither one spoke.

With each passing day the burden of their sabotage had grown heavier. The inner turmoil showed on their faces. Lydia and Stan had commented at supper about their lack of appetite, but had not pushed them with questions. Even exercising the horses had become a chore. Summer, glorious summer, dulled. They almost wished for the robotic routines and boring schedules of school—anything so that they would no longer have to think about what they did and what could happen to them because of it.

"Maybe we should tell Ma and Pop," Jake sighed. "Maybe we should just get it over with. Better than dreading the news every day and jumping every time someone telephones."

Maya turned a page in her sketchbook and began a new drawing. "Maybe we should."

"Yeah, maybe we should," Jake repeated.

Another silence overtook them, punctuated only by Maya's faint pencil scratchings and Jake's periodic sighs.

"We need to make some new plans, Jake."

"Yeah, I know. Too bad I'm brain dead."

"What can we do?" Maya was talking as much to herself as to Jake. "What can we do to undo what we did?"

"If only we could undo .... " Jake halted midsentence and bolted upright.

Maya whirled to face him. " ... undo what we did!"

By midnight plans were set. The next afternoon they went to town with Lydia, saddle money in their pockets, and bought engine oil from five different places. They concealed it under a tarpaulin in the back of the pick-up.

"Don't look under the tarp, okay Ma? We're working on a surprise project."

It was too late by the time Lydia finished work for them to carry out phase two of the plan, but they managed to unload the oil without Stan or Lydia seeing it, and later that night they skulked around the barn to prepare the packs for the next day's ride. They stashed the packs out of sight in the ditch a short distance from the ranch.

The next morning Stan was intently framing the kitchen addition and Lydia was thinning carrots when the saboteurs trotted Felix and Hannah out of the paddock and down the lane.

"Have a nice ride, kids," Stan called to them.

Maya and Jake picked up the stashed packs from the ditch. It was an awkward ride up Blue Diamond Road because they had to juggle the clumsy packs of oil and tools in front of them on the saddles. They rode past the Junction and went as close as they could to the logging camp trailer without danger of being heard or seen by Steve and Al. There they left the containers of oil and their tools carefully camouflaged by the overgrown railroad track. Merrily they cantered home.

"Well, old buddy, old pal, ready for the dawn ride tomorrow?" Jake was again stretched out on the bed as Maya sat drawing at her table.

Maya did not reply, nor did Jake expect one. It was nice to be at ease, to be almost carefree again, to have lazy non-conversations and to think of nothing in particular.

"So what are you drawing, Maya?"

"I'll show you in a few minutes."

What Maya had done was to draw scenes from her dream flights. There was the cave, the baby bigfoot clinging to her, the hidden hot springs and the bigfeet luxuriating in the warm water and on the smooth surrounding rocks.

"Yowie, those are good!"

"I was thinking about what Nina said the other night. You know, about education. If only people like Mrs. Stottle and Ida Jones and maybe even Sidder could see what we saw, then maybe they'd change their minds."

"You're a gen-u-ine genius, Maya. I love the punk haircut on the baby."

"I was trying to write stuff underneath the pictures, but it sounds too icky or weird. If only I could make them talk."

"Why don't you, Maya. Make them talk! Just put bubbles over their heads, like in comics."

"Jake! A bigfoot comic!" Ideas sparked and flashed between the two. "Maybe Eliot would put it in the *Valley Times*! Will you help me? Want to do it together?"

"Yeah, we could make it a series, you know, and leave off just when the action gets good."

"Then people will want to see the next installment. We could call it ... 'To Be Continued,' or something like, 'The Continuing Adventures of Little Bigfoot.'"

"Or, 'Baby Bigfoot Goes to Jail for Draining Oil from Caterpillars.' Or, 'Bigfoot Punk in

Trouble Again.'" Jake erupted in giggles. "'Bigfoot Punk Wets Top Bunk.'"

Maya magnified the silliness, and soon they were lying on the floor, clutching their stomachs as they guffawed and choked out one ridiculous title after another. And though their own continuing adventure began at dawn, Maya and Jake were wide awake late into the brief midsummer's night.

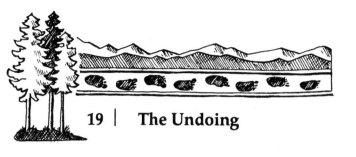

19 | The Undoing

Maya and Jake had chosen dawn as the best time for undoing their sabotage because they knew that people who drank as much beer as Steve and Al did were often dopey in the morning. They left a note on the kitchen table saying they were going for an early ride and silently got the horses ready, leaving the halters on underneath the bridles. They walked Felix and Hannah out of earshot of the house and then cantered up Blue Diamond Road past the Junction. The dew-drenched packs of tools and oil were just where they had left them. They removed the horses' bridles and tethered Felix and Hannah so they could graze while they worked on the machines.

Carting the packs on their backs up the old spur was harder than they had planned. By the time they were within range of the machines in the turn-around yard, the sun had angled over Narnauk Peak to the northeast and bathed the Valley with a new day.

The first machine—Johnnie's D7H—had its oil intake underneath the engine cover, just where it should have been according to the diagram in the road construction journal. Maya and Jake crawled up and over the tractor, lifted the metal plate, and there it was. Using Lydia's First Law of Opening Jars, Maya wrapped a rag around the oil cap and twisted. Off came the cap. Jake poured in the oil.

What had been to their advantage when they had drained the machines was now distinctly to their disadvantage—they were working in full view of the trailer, up on top of the yellow machines, not hidden underneath them. They replaced the engine cover, picked up the empty oil containers, and moved to the second machine.

"Dang," Jake whispered. "Where is it?"

"These are the spark plugs so this is the engine block. Here it is."

Jake unscrewed the oil cap. Maya reached for a container of oil.

"Get down, Jake."

They flattened themselves against the grader's metal walkway, their jeans and shirts conspicuous against the yellow background.

One of the guards, Steve, opened the trailer door and stepped out. He was wearing underwear—a tee-shirt and shorts. He walked stiffly to the side of the trailer and urinated into the bushes. Without even glancing around, he returned to the trailer and shut the door.

"He's gone back to bed," Maya whispered.

"Yeah. Cripes, I must have dropped the cap." Jake climbed down off the grader and searched underneath it. "Maya—it's not here. Look in the engine."

Maya muttered Lydia's First Law of Finding Things, "If I were an oil cap where would I be?"

"Jake! Here it is!"

Jake climbed back up onto the grader. The engine glugged eight litres.

"It doesn't seem like enough, Maya. What if the engines seize up after all?"

"They won't." Maya was down off the grader, piling the empty containers behind the berm and fetching more. Jake scrambled after her.

They needed a wrench to get the oil cap open on the third machine. Minutes ticked by each time they stopped to check the trailer, and each cautious movement took twice the time a normal action would take. The sun warmed up the locusts, cicadas and other insects, who began their summer background buzzing and chirring. Soon Al and Steve would feel the sun's heat inside the trailer and wake up, if only to open doors and windows.

"We've got to move more quickly!" Maya's eyes stung with sweat. Her skin was crawling. "If we make it through this, Jake, I'll never again .... " Maya was not sure what she planned never again to do. It had something to do with mistaking outings like this with excitement and adventure. There was nothing exciting about what they were doing; it was agonizing and deadening.

"Yeah, I know. Not like the movies, eh, Maya?"

The oil cap on the fourth machine was frozen. Even with the pipe extension it would not budge. Jake scrambled to the packs behind the turn-around berm and returned with a can of WD-40. They sprayed the cap and left it to soak and moved on to replenish the oil in the fifth and last machine they had sabotaged.

"Come on, Machine God," Jake whispered. "Open and receive our gift." The fifth machine was easy. They returned to the packs to leave empties and pick up the last full containers.

"Number Four, please oh please, Number Four .... " Maya and Jake placed the wrench over the oil cap and pulled. It did not budge. They placed the pipe extension over the handle of the wrench and once again pulled with all their might. Nothing.

"Move around on the other side, Maya. I'll get my feet braced. You push. I'll pull."

If they could have grunted and shouted with exertion, the cap might have budged, but having to work silently cramped their style.

"Okay," Maya whispered. "Let's spritz it again and wait a few minutes."

The trailer door opened and Al stepped out under the awning. He stood scratching and yawning for a moment before walking a short distance to the Johnny-on-the-Spot.

Maya and Jake slid off the Caterpillar and hid by its enormous back tires to wait for Al to emerge from the portable toilet and return to the trailer.

"He's in. Let's go."

Once again they climbed up and this time the cap came loose. In their rush oil slopped on them and dribbled down into the engine. They replaced the cap, grabbed the tools and slid to the ground, limp with exertion. Adrenalin rushes had left them feeble.

"I'll take the tools," Jake whispered. "You get the empties."

A cloud of dust and the roar of an engine flattened them behind the D7H, just a few metres from the protection of the berm. They were so close! All they had to do was get over the berm, pack the tools and empties and get back down the tracks to Felix and Hannah.

Up the mine road bounced a pickup. It halted by the trailer and Johnnie Stottle got out.

Johnnie's eyes lovingly scanned the machines, one by one. Though Sidder was paying him during the delay, driving water up to the camp and doing odd jobs around Sidder's city headquarters did not suit Johnnie. He was growing restless. He wanted to be driving, building the roads, or snaking logs with the diesel-powered winch up to the giant crane. Or driving the crane and loading logs like toothpicks onto waiting trucks.

"You two dead in there or what?"

Johnnie lounged against the pickup for a moment, waiting for a response from within the trailer, and then he started across the turn-around yard towards the D7H Cat. Maya and Jake shrank. They pressed bodies and faces into the dry loose clay from which the thin layer of topsoil had been scraped when Johnnie had levelled the yard.

Johnnie swung up into the cab of the grader. They heard little clanking noises and then a series of clicks. A few moments later the engine burst into sound. Johnnie had started it up! Would he back up or go forward? Maya and Jake prepared to spring clear and run. Concern about the amount of replacement oil vanished. Time stood still.

Johnnie dismounted, leaving the grader running, and went to the next machine. Jake and Maya's muscles shook and jerked uncontrollably.

Johnnie swung into the second cab and in a few moments the bulldozer leaped to life. Johnnie went down the row of machines, started them all, and ambled towards the trailer.

Steve and Al were now outside, standing with mugs in hand, watching Johnnie. When the three of them sat in lawn chairs to talk and drink coffee, Maya and Jake backed up like crayfish, on their bellies in the dirt, no longer needing to worry about the noise they made. One at a time they chose a moment to heave themselves over the berm.

Neither one recalled much about the race back to the horses and the flight home.

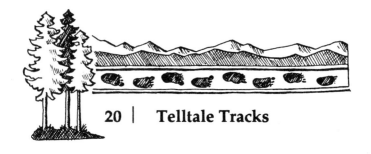

20 | Telltale Tracks

Maya and Jake worked on their bigfoot comic every day for hours at a time. Lydia and Stan were pleased to see them cheerful again and so at first said nothing about how much of the precious fair weather they were spending inside, how there would be plenty of rainy days for indoor projects.

After they made an outline and a rough draft of the entire story, they divided the story into eight-frame sections. They wanted to complete two episodes before they talked with Eliot about the possibility his printing the comic in *The Kagitwa Valley Times*. To make each episode interesting enough in only eight frames was more difficult than they imagined. Although there were times when they grew frustrated with the project, they never lost the initial excitement. Now that they had undone their dirty work, life seemed so simple and fresh that their writing frustrations never lasted very long.

When they were satisfied with the story for the first two installments, Maya did drawings in pencil and inked them in with a new pen. They were ready. They called Eliot and arranged an appointment for the next afternoon when Lydia went to work. Only then did they show their parents what they had done.

Lydia and Stan reacted quite differently to the comic. Lydia grew silent and almost tearful. In a voice so low they strained to hear, she said, "This is miraculous."

Stan's reaction was to laugh boisterously and heap praise on them for the clever drawings and storyline. He asked all the right questions, the main one of which was, "What happens next?"

"Parents always like their children's art," Maya told Jake later. "Let's not crash and burn."

"Right," said Jake. "Consider me chilled out."

Eliot Thompson's reaction to the comic strip was first to chuckle and then to ask, "Where'd you two find this material?"

"Uh, we just uh .... " Jake stuttered.

Maya completed his sentence. "We just dreamed it up."

"Okay. We'll run the first strip in Wednesday's paper, with a notice by it for readers to call the office if they'd like to see what happens next. If you get ten calls, we'll run the second installment the following week. I'll pay you from strip two on. How's that? And no fair getting your friends to call in. You'd better find a *nom de plume*."

Maya and Jake floated on air all the rest of that day and night. Wednesday morning they were posted at the end of the lane by the mailbox. With shaking hands they opened the newspaper. And there it was! A real comic in a real newspaper, for all the world to see. They stared unbelieving at their invention.

The crash and burn came soon enough.

Would ten people be curious about the next installment, curious enough to telephone the *Valley Times*? Would anyone bother? Should they call Eliot now to see if any earlybirds had telephoned? Should they call the Morrisons to see if they had read the newspaper yet? They pestered Stan and Lydia with endless questions and suppositions, and irritated them during breakfast by jumping up and down to look again at the newspaper which they had lovingly spread out on the living room desk. Half a dozen times either Jake or Maya would go to the telephone, lift the receiver, and put it down again.

Stan finally took the situation in hand. "Since you two can't figure out a constructive way to spend your day, how about helping me with the addition?"

He worked them hard all morning, with only a few minutes' break for lunch. They were happy when the nails ran out and Stan had to go to town for more. They dashed into the house and glued themselves to the telephone.

"And it looks like a couple of kids was crawling around the machines. There's tracks all over the place. Somebody was messing with a few of the engines. Might be the same girl and boy we saw hiking a couple of weeks ago. The boy couldn't talk. Girl said he was her cousin. Someone said you had a couple of kids and kept horses. There's hoof prints all over the lower part of the road."

Steve stood on the verandah, talking with Lydia. She had heard someone drive in the lane, but had not bothered to interrupt her garden work. Stan had gone to town for nails, but Maya and Jake were in the house. Exasperated by the persistent knocking, Lydia finally had left the garden and gone around to the front of the house to see who was there.

Now Steve stood with his back to the screened door.

"Well, our daughter and son certainly do ride the Blue Diamond Road. They often exercise the horses there. As far as I know there's public access up to the Junction."

Out of the corner of her eye Lydia noticed Maya and Jake slink out of the front room.

"Well, missus, there's five million dollars worth of equipment at the camp. We're just warning you in case it's your kids snooping around. We're authorized to use guns. That's private property. Sidder didn't hire us to let vandals mess up his investment. We'd hate anybody to get hurt."

Lydia could not quite piece together the information. A boy who could not talk? Who on earth was that? A girl and her cousin? Why had the children slunk out of view of the stranger? Lydia shelved her mystery-solving compulsion in order to speak to the visitor.

"Well, thank you for taking the trouble to stop by, Mr. ... "

"Steve. Steven Rusk. Just call me Steve."

"Pleased to meet you, Steve. I'm Lydia. Lydia Langhorne." Lydia held out her hand, but just as Steve put out his own in an automatic response to her, she retracted hers. It was an awkward moment.

"Oh, I'm sorry!" Lydia laughed. "I'm covered with dirt!"

"Don't matter," Steve said.

"Anyway," Lydia continued. "I certainly am glad you came by and I'll speak to the children right away to make sure they know the boundaries of Mr. Sidder's land. Thanks again."

Steve mumbled that he had better get going, and left. Lydia returned to the garden. Half an hour passed before Jake and Maya appeared before her, sheepish and scared.

"We have something to tell you," Maya began.

" ... that you might not like," Jake continued.

Lydia's eyes pierced and silenced them. She came to the edge of the garden and stood for a long moment saying nothing. How they wished they could roll back time so they would not have to face this moment with Lydia. They had broken her trust. They who were allowed to go hiking and riding on their own. They who had freedoms and privileges envied by most of their school friends. Stan and Lydia did not pry into their affairs—they trusted them and so refrained from questions. And now, now they would confess their deeds and ever after have lost the trust so carefully built over the years.

Neither Maya nor Jake felt like crying. Instead they felt helpless and lost. They felt the same weakness as when Jenny had died. Their faithful old dog died and they wanted to have her back, to have her romp with them, follow them wherever they went, curl up on the rug and read with them. They felt powerless now, just as they had when all their wishing could not bring Jenny back from being dead.

"Your twelfth summer," Lydia said. "Well, I guess your twelfth summer is not too early for you to learn one of the big secrets of the adult world." Lydia sighed wistfully. "Something my mother never let me in on."

Jake and Maya waited, each filtering through how much of the sabotage operation they would have to tell, wondering if the whole thing would spill out as soon as they started talking.

"Maya and Jake, there are some things which are better left unsaid."

Lydia turned back to the garden and continued where she had left off staking up tomatoes. Maya and Jake stood expectantly for a few minutes, before quietly moving away. In the cool dark of the stable loft, they talked.

"She still trusts us," Maya said. "It was our business and we took care of it and she doesn't want to know about it."

"She still trusts us," Jake echoed. "Do you think she knows? What did she mean?"

Brother and sister lay on bales of fragrant new hay.

"Sometime I want to tell Ma and Pop about our bigfoot dreams and about what we did to Sidder's machines," Maya said after a profound silence.

"Me, too," Jake said. "But not right away. Because, uh, because it seems kind of like a secret between us and the sasquatch, if you know what I mean."

With Jake's words Maya hit a new level of release. "Jake, that's exactly it! We would be breaking trust with the bigfeet if we told. Ma and Pop have to dream the bigfeet for themselves!"

Jake smiled. He loved praise from his older sister, even if she was not that much older. "Yeah, well, what can I say? I'm a gen-u-ine genius."

Jake pulled his gen-u-ine Stetson down over his ears and rolled on the baled hay the way Jenny used to, scratching her back and kicking in ecstacy. Maya grabbed the knotted rope which dangled at the edge of the stable loft and swung out over the barn floor.

"Just thought of something, Maya." Jake sat up. "Aren't we telling the secret through the comic strip? I mean, it's there for the whole world to read. Isn't the comic strip breaking trust?"

Maya pushed off when her feet touched the packed bales on the other side of the barn and came flying back over the stable loft. "Naw. That's fiction."

Summer once again was filled with promise. There were so many things to do—exercise the horses, make plans with Karen and Sam for their overnighter, explore the places they had seen in dream flight—so many things to do and so many endless summer days to do them in.

It was a curious thing how nearly every magazine Maya and Jake picked up, every radio program, every book which caught their eyes in the library or bookstore had something to do with logging or mythical creatures or land management or native relationships to living things. Everywhere they turned they encountered information about the very things which now interested them.

"Hey, listen to this." The family was once again in the living room at the end of a day. Stan was refining his kitchen plan, Lydia had her feet propped on the arm of his chair, reading another mystery, and Jake and Maya lay on the floor, surrounded by books from the most recent foray to the library.

"'The natives who lived on the Pacific coast of North America, like most other in-dig— indig—indig-en-us people ....'"

"Indigenous," Maya inserted.

"' ... like most other indigenous people,'" Jake continued, "'found individual ownership of land to be an alien concept.'"

After a moment's pause, they all returned to their own private worlds. The mantle clock ticked comfortingly. Through an open window the last birds chirped their goodnights and a breeze rustled the leaves of aspen Lydia had planted near the house.

"Hah! Gawley's the culprit!" Lydia muttered.

Maya was rereading *Charlotte's Web*, something she did every summer. "Listen to this." She read aloud a passage which held new meaning for her: "'Life is a rich and steady time when you are waiting for something to happen or to hatch.'"

Again, everyone paused to listen, and many thoughts were generated by E.B. White's words. Stan drifted into a reverie about the new barn he would build. Lydia floated back to her birch tree and the evening she had stayed late, sure that the root spirits would reveal themselves to her. Jake thought of the bigfoot picnic and decided that tonight he would dream fly back to the stone circle. And Maya also thought of the bigfeet, of the way the baby felt in her arms. She wondered if she would ever discover the secret of their reality.

The telephone rang. Everyone jumped.

"I'll get it." Maya was first to her feet.

It was Eliot. "We're rolling the next install-ment," he told her. "And you two better get busy and cook up a bunch more strips. The phone is ringing off the hook. Your bizarre lit-tle character seems to have struck some chord with Valley readers."

THE ADVENTURES OF LITTLE BIGFOOT

By Hannah Felix

Part One

But they LOOK friendly – kinda like us, only silly and bald. Let's get one to follow us home. Then we could play with it!

JUST take our word for it – they're dangerous. It was different before the GREAT SEPARATION. Don't cross into their world, little Bigfoot. HEED OUR WARNING!

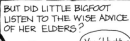

BUT DID LITTLE BIGFOOT LISTEN TO THE WISE ADVICE OF HER ELDERS?

You'd better stay here coyote.

... OF COURSE NOT!! Little Bigfoot wanted to find out for herself about these strange creatures called humans.

C'mon Sweetgrass

First thing I need is some body bark and a head shelf like humans wear.

LATER...

Hey! That must be the new kid! Wanna play?

Humans are not so bad, are they Sweetgrass?

BUT, Little Bigfoot did not know what lay in store for her THAT VERY NIGHT!!!

TO BE CONTINUED...

OTHER BOOKS FOR YOUNG READERS
BY DEIRDRE KESSLER

Lena and the Whale
Spike Chiseltooth
Home for Christmas
Lobster in my Pocket
The Private Adventures of Brupp
Brupp on the Other Side
Brupp in the Land of Snow
Brupp Rides Again

IN FRENCH:

Lina et la baleine
Un homard dans ma poche

Some of Deirdre Kessler's books are also available
in foreign language editions.

DISTRIBUTED IN CANADA BY:

General Publishing
30 Lesmill Road
Don Mills, Ontario
Canada M3B 2T6